FROLIC

ON THE

AMARANTHYN

CHASE A. FOLMAR

SABLE STAR PRESS

FROLIC ON THE AMARANTHYN

Copyright © 2022 by Chase A. Folmar

All rights reserved.

Cover art by Goran Gligović

Title design by Nonpolygon

A Sable Star Press Book

Library of Congress Control Number: 2022902469

ISBN 979-8-9856902-0-0 (Paperback)
ISBN 979-8-9856902-1-7 (eBook)

to Rhianne and my family,
without whose help this
wouldn't have been possible.

FROLIC
ON THE
AMARANTHYN

There are beings - and artifacts - against which we batter our intelligence raw, and in the end make peace with reality only by saying, "It was an apparition, a thing of beauty and horror."
—Gene Wolfe, *The Claw of the Conciliator*

I

THE cadaverons were defeated.

Whereas the lonely mountain road had swarmed only moments prior with those exhumed and worm-rotted effigies of dead men, what remained of their gruesomeness now lay hacked in scattered heaps across the uneven path. Knots of necromantic twine, whose repellent touch had spurred disparate pieces of flesh into so paltry an imitation of life, were left sundered in uselessly twitching strands, unable to further animate the figures whom they had previously bound.

A small company of armed men stood in the aftermath of that slaughter. Bloodied and haggard of breath, each counted himself lucky to have survived so sudden an ambush along the mountain path. Wrapped like the coils of a great python around slopes flung indomitably up towards the darkening sky, the narrow road had nearly choked them in its grasp when the flood of rot-riddled figures came clawing and gnashing with mindless fervor upon them, providing precious little space to mount a defense against an otherwise easily conquered foe.

Now, with victory at length claimed, they warily gathered round the armored carriage in whose service they had marched these many days gone by, stealing hearty gulps from both waterskins and flasks aflame with more tempestuous spirits alike. Little was spoken, the lot reeling from so harrowing an encounter, while thoughts of warm food, soft beds, and bawdy company to be enjoyed at the end of this journey filled the prolonged silence between them.

There then came from the cover of nearby trees a sudden rustling in the brush. Weapons drawn and leveled in anticipation for another threat, the men were thusly taken aback to see not a beast or conjured fiend emerge before them, but a woman. She appeared as if a goddess who deigned to tread the same ground as lowly mortals, stunning in the beauty she exuded, fair and supple as calla lilies in bloom, a scant dress of cerulean silk flowing down her figure. Without a moment's hesitation, she proceeded to skip about the cluster of men, showering each of their cheeks with a flurry of eager and passionately insistent kisses.

"Such heroes! Such brave defenders of the helpless!" Like a well-rehearsed song did her praises ring, from lips glistening potently with a darkly crimson sheen as she continued to extoll their company. "What fortune must stand by my side, that Fate brought you to this road at precisely when I most needed aide! I know not how much longer I could have stayed hidden, helpless to fight those fiends who so ruthlessly pursued me, before your company came around the bend, a gallant force with swords and spears and steadfast shields. How glorious it was to see you slay creatures so foul as they! I knew I would find safety in your hands; and so I have!"

None of the battle-weathered men responded. With porcelain saucer eyes they followed the swaying hips and flourishes of her shapely form as she danced between them, her crown of golden hair seeming to catch with every bounce those last splendid breaths of sunlight still peeking out over the horizon. Though entranced by this unexpected surprise, they were, after all, mercenaries by trade, whose loyalty lay only in that shining god of golden coin. Tempting as this woman was, they had no wish to incur their employer's displeasure by stepping beyond the parameters of previously ascribed duties, and so knew not how to proceed with the pleasantness of her arrival.

It was as if the sheer radiance of her smile, and the ruby marks left behind by her kisses, had resulted in a sort of shared amnesia to the battle they had but recently escaped, and which had cut an initial force of fifteen men at arms to a paltry eight. Likewise, none sought to question the reason as to why one so seemingly frail and unprepared for the wilderness had found her way to such a spot, nor how she had come to be pursued by the cadaverons in the first place.

Such a spell of blindness, however, could not be said to have fallen over the entire company. One of their number, who'd born the rank of captain when there had been a full retinue to command, yet retained some semblance of the situation at hand, so that when the woman's lips grazed his own weathered face, it snapped through the lure her presence had previously induced, and his expression darkened to an incredulous grimace.

"Enough!" he barked. "What is your business here, woman?"

She stared at him with the innocence of one scolded for an impropriety they had unknowingly and ignorantly trespassed upon. "Must I beg for forgiveness at having occupied the wrong place at the wrong time? Is it a crime to have been hunted by evil and unnatural forces I know not from whence came, or for what purpose they were brought into being? Shall I proceed on alone down this path falling swiftly under the spell of shadows now, after having so narrowly escaped Death, and pray my luck hold strong against all the forces of nightly wilderness?"

The captain could but scowl in return, for at that moment a hatch sealing shut one of the carriage windows swung open and allowed the portly visage of a sallow-faced man to peer through.

"The danger is passed?"

By the vibrant raiment and the garish coiffure sprouted atop his head, it was apparent the speaker was a eupatrid born of white-shored Iskalruun. Though fervid insistence burned in beady eyes scouring the grisly aftermath of battle, his voice still squawked with a shrill and trembling tenor, betraying the nervousness clearly buried so shallowly beneath. Though his fiery gaze alighted first upon the mercenary captain, it was only a matter of seconds before that blaze drifted to the woman beside him; to long locks fluttering with the breeze across a striking, heart-shaped face, and a dress, wonderfully delicate in design, which hugged tight all those places to best attract a wandering eye. The smoldering ire softened, and an ember of a different sort was quickly stoked in its place. "Hello, hello! Who is this that so graces us with her presence?"

"One who is eternally grateful unto you, venerable liege," the woman eagerly approached the window with her most reverent, most alluring gait, as if she had expected his appearance all along, and curtseyed low when she stood before him. With eyes sparkling like the ocean beneath a cloudless summer day did she entreat the eupatrid into their full and shimmering depths, and she beamed brighter still as she addressed him. "I offer my name as Emrasarie, woeful traveler along these isolated roads. I owe my life to your swordsmen for the role they played in my rescue, and to you, perhaps even more so, for having brought them here at my hour of need. Were it not for your arrival, I would no doubt have perished only moments ago!"

"Let us thank Fate that such misfortune did not befall one so beautiful as you!" grinned the eupatrid as he drank in the sight of her. "Many before have lauded the gracious and benefactory quality of my name, which I am pleased to offer as Aresh Lonnaskae. It warms my heart that you are now among those who know its quality as well."

Emrasarie gave a bashful chirp of laughter. Before she could further weave her flattery, however, the mercenary captain lumbered forward, and sidestepped around to speak directly with the enraptured eupatrid.

"Eminency, nightfall will be upon us soon," he spoke tersely, all the while glancing at Emrasarie from the corner of his eye. "We are yet several hours at least from Lucrauna, and unless we wish to sleep beneath the stars tonight, I would council we make towards civilization with haste, before the wilds of the Ingrolith Mountains rise fully against our progress."

Aresh Lonnaskae, his gaze momentarily stolen from Emrasarie, looked out across the waiting road ahead and gave a nod in return.

As if fearful of his attention slipping further adrift, Emrasarie then threw herself forward beneath the eupatrid's window, clasping her hands together in hopeful supplication.

"Pardon my intrusion," she began anew, "but did I hear your destination to be Lucrauna? So was it mine, before those cadaverons fell against me. Perchance, most-gracious eminency, might I request the honor of travelling alongside your retinue, until at least we reach the city? I will be off my own way then at once, never to disturb the path of your travels again."

Mounting distrust narrowed the captain's eyes, though did not seem to trouble Emrasarie in the least; she was cognizant of the eupatrid's face only, and when there passed a leer of self-satisfied amusement across the man's heavy jowls at her request, so too did a smile similar in-kind flash across the fullness of her own cheeks.

"Your appearance is no disturbance, but an honor to my company!" Aresh Lonnaskae bellowed brightly from atop his seat. "Please, after such an experience as you have endured, share in what little comfort I might provide and ride with me for the remainder of our journey."

Locks were unclasped, knobs jostled, and the heavy plated door of the carriage then swung ajar. Yet before Emrasarie could take a single step forward, the captain swooped between, barring her way with a hand that had found its way to the hilt of his blade.

"Is that wise, Eminency? We know not what this woman's intentions may be, or the reason we happened to find her here. By her own words it was she the cadaverons so ruthlessly pursued. What if ill-omens flock about her, and she draws towards our weakened band more misfortune than we can manage?"

Aresh Lonnaskae loosed an indignant scoff at the presented notion and swatted flippantly at the air. "Bah, cease such inane prattle! Can you not see this woman is helpless here amidst the wilderness? Now, step aside and allow her to enter. You would not desire your payment to reflect any insubordination of my wishes now, would you?"

Talk of golden-faced crioses, particularly the threat of their quantity being in any way diminished, quelled immediately the captain's defiance. With resigned loyalty did he step aside, and Aresh Lonnaskae leaned down to offer Emrasarie his hand in a grand show of gallantry.

The golden-haired woman performed her own masterpiece in turn, taking with sweet and charming flourish those bloated fingers stuffed into the grip of so many gem-studded rings.

The carriage interior had space enough to fit four comfortably, and was lavishly decorated with periwinkle cushions and pillowed seats embroidered in Sundranalli silk. Her smile unwavering, Emrasarie followed the guiding pull of her host and dropped to the seat beside him. All the while did her sing-song voice dance about in thanks and gratitude, and she made certain to offer forth her forgiveness in lacking those proper forms of etiquette so refined a eupatrid as he no doubt cherished. Swept along by the disarming sincerity of her words, Aresh Lonnaskae's own tone fell into that self-assured air of vanity as befalls so many to whom rank and status has been blindly given, and he assured her, as one might a child woefully unlearned in the esoteric rules of some complex game, that no impropriety could ever be committed by one so lovely as her.

Thusly secure in the carriage, the eupatrid bid his company to carry on towards their destination, bringing out from a drawer overhead a small cask of wine and several glasses as he did.

The captain scowled with brazen displeasure at the sight of Emrasarie visible there through the open window, the heavy lines on his face only just able to hide a faint tinge of red creeping along the cheek which she had earlier kissed. Catching his lingering stare upon her, the woman cast a coquettish wave his direction before he spun and lumbered off ahead.

II

Twilight presently fell upon them. Its rolling waves of violet splashed over the looming snow-dusted peaks of the Ingroliths, and flooded down precarious slopes arching high on every side, bathing deep the road in hues akin to the dusky wine that flowed unrestrained within the carriage. Holding up her glass for yet another toast, Emrasarie glanced out the small window, and marked how far across its empyrean path red-rivered Merexiol had traversed since the eupatrid welcomed her with unsuspecting arms into his convoy. From its perch just above the serrated horizon, she inferred little more than an hour had transpired since then; an hour since she had kissed each of his remaining band of hired mercenaries.

She hid an eager grin while sipping lightly at the rim of her cup.

Beside her, already awash in the crimson light of that nearest moon, Aresh Lonnaskae's face flushed darker still as he guzzled down the entirety of what had just been poured, his rounded cheeks fit to burst like a pair of fully-ripened cherries. With his sleeve he wiped away a trail of wine gone slithering down the expanse of his swollen jowls, either ignorant or unconcerned by the stain it left there, before shuffling ever so slightly in his seat closer to her. It was with a flawlessly crafted mask Emrasarie continued to smile even as those swollen fingers crept around her waist.

It had been many years since the mask had forced its way upon her face. A lifetime ago, it sometimes seemed, when men whose coin flashed as deadly as the bared teeth of hungry wolves had found her in the underbelly of Byrethlia's slums, alone and abandoned by parents either too poor, too cruel, or too dead to bother with her any longer. Into the service of their licentious chains had she then been ensnared, blinded by promises of protection and profit they so readily offered, realizing too late the steep price she had paid, her well-being guaranteed only so long as it brought pleasure to paying clients and coin to her masters' coffers.

What choice did she thereby have other than to create so alluring and reliable an illusion? It was in the pursuit of survival she had perfected the flutter of her lashes, the way she twirled at her hair, the curl of her lips into a smile, able to wield her fabricated face with the same proficiency a renowned swordsman might their famous blade. Even now, long since she had slashed the throat of her last, most odious client and escaped the clutches of so wretched an existence, she sometimes still surprised herself at how easily the mask fell back in place, and how effortlessly men like Aresh Lonnaskae were cajoled by the wicked weapon that was her charm.

Still, a thief and brigand as herself must be willing to use each and every advantage when it came to the prying of treasured valuables from guarded hands. So she bat her lashes, twirled her hair, and beamed wide her smile at every word the eupatrid spoke, guiding their talk down winding currents of idle conversation in pursuit of those exact places she desired them to reach. Of those subjects that might resolve him towards reticence did she masterfully steer clear from, while she stoked faster and with gentle pushes those that would endear her further in his eyes, bolstering his willingness to share those precious secrets he would have otherwise kept closely guarded to his chest.

It was not a task that required exceeding strain. Aresh Lonnaskae mirrored almost every client she had been subjected to while in service of her masters: little more than meek husks once the fierce and illustrious trappings of societal rank had been shorn, supported but by the braggadocious heat of their own breath, and the perceived infallibility inherited power had armored them with since before their own feet could support them. Power which, more often than not, cast in its wake expansive and pecuniary shadows.

"It is a sad state Iskalruun has fallen to which led me to abandon its proud and ancient walls," he lamented after another heavy draught of wine, finally broaching the subject which Emrasarie was most interested in with wistful eyes and words that fell sloppily from his lips. "The strength and influence of the old houses are gone, ever since that damnable sorceress crowned herself as queen, and stripped away generations of tradition in favor of her

11

own rule. It was intolerable, dwelling while hampered by the whims of her fanatic adherents, and ever-watched beneath the ire of sorcerous eyes she sent to burn through the sky at all times. I could bear it no longer, and so mustered what I could from long-unopened vaults and set out upon the wider world, eager for a new home to make my own."

"A grand fortune it must be to have spurred so daring an endeavor! And wonderfully hidden too, for I have seen not a hint of chests or burdened coffers since stepping within your carriage. Any thieves who might fall upon you would likely think their schemes ruined when unable to find any of the treasure they so duplicitously covet!"

"Ah, my dear! I carry something *far* more valuable than trinkets of gold, silver, or even precious orichalcum." His face twisting in a mischievous grin, Aresh Lonnaskae leaned over and pulled open a secret compartment built beneath the carriage floor. For the brief moment he held the lid ajar, Emrasarie saw a wide and shallow iron case sealed by little more than a latch along its face.

"Though oaths given compel me to secrecy, I can say it is like no other worldly treasure, something which my family unknowingly held for countless generations, lost within the vaults of the ancestral house, and yet so valuable even the damnable Queen Empyreal herself would pay dearly to possess it. Indeed, I make for Lucrauna now at the behest of a *very* interested prospective client, who, if the rumors are to be believed, will bestow upon me riches beyond even the scope of kings for its conveyance unto them."

So gluttonous was the fire which gleamed in the eupatrid's eyes, even after the compartment had been resealed and his attention brought back upon her, that Emrasarie found herself momentarily entranced by its intensity, reveling in the thought of soon holding such a prize in her own hands. Straining to even conceive of what riches he could be hinting at, she noted it was nearly time for the next stage of their plan to begin, and so maintained her role as ingratiated flatterer for the time being.

"The city will glow brighter still with one so noble as you within it," was all she said.

"Yes, a place of beauty to be sure, and one I hope will satiate my needs for a time once such vast wealth flows from my fingers. Tell me, have you heard whisper of Numynaris's Ark, and the Frolic said to carry on without end upon it? Have you ever dreamed-"

Whatever Aresh Lonnaskae might have said next was interrupted by a guttural wail from outside. Almost immediately another joined the first, then another, and another still, until a full chorus of agony shrieked from all eight mouths that remained around them. Quickly did their tenor grow hoarse as the source of their assault did not cease, and in fact seemed to harshen.

This time, she did not attempt to smother the smile curling at her lips as the carriage jolted to a stop.

"My mercenaries!" Aresh Lonnaskae gasped as he peeked out the carriage windows. His eyes bulged wide in shock, while the sanguine shroud of intoxication he had worn but a moment prior was stolen from his face. "What has overcome them? They are all bent over in pain, clawing and scratching at their faces! It looks as if they can hardly stand! Wait, there's something out there; something moving through the woods. Oh, oh no!"

Setting her wine aside, Emrasarie shed the relaxed slouch she had affected and straightened to the alert posture of a predator poised on the verge of attack. With long white fingers she tussled at her saffron locks and smoothed the creases of her dress, all while ignoring the eupatrid as he threw shut the window's hatch and cowered low amidst his cushions. Secure though they were behind a locked and plated shell, the carriage walls could not dampen the sudden clamor of steel striking steel that rang out with cold, ferocious notes, and Emrasarie followed intently the scream of the newly-added ninth blade as it swung about the fray.

Through attempted parries did its weight shatter like thunder ripping the sky asunder. The breaking of corslets rang out as if poultry bones being crushed underfoot, and one by one were those wailing cries of Aresh Lonnaskae's mercenaries severed short.

As each body crumbled to the ground in a heavy thud, Emrasarie murmured a silent ode of thanks; not for the benefit of whatever nameless listener might happen to hear, but for her own assurance during this final stage in the gamble she and her beloved had orchestrated.

At length there remained but a single mercenary between them and the attacker. His stertorous breath cut horribly through the resulting lull left by the newcomer's sword, and Emrasarie laughed to herself upon hearing his steps fumble up towards the carriage.

"Help!" the man could but pitifully wheeze, his face no doubt inflamed and corroded past recognition from the rhogalida venom left there in the shape of her pursed lips. "Let me in, I beg you! I cannot-"

His plea was unceremoniously silenced by the cleaving of flesh, sinew, and bone. The song of Death as had culled the remainder of the mercenary company rang no more, and its sudden absence echoed with the sheer ruthlessness by which their number had so thoroughly been decimated.

Aresh Lonnaskae, surely aware of how dire his chances at survival had become, sank even lower within the carriage seats, and clutched feebly at his pillows as if they might shield him from harm.

"Are you armed, eminency?" spoke Emrasarie softly. She leaned close to him, so close she could see the thin tufts of hair about his ears rustling with her breath, and smell the wine-soaked sweat trickling down his face.

"Alas, I am defenseless," he whispered, and took hold her hand as if to provide comfort. "Yet fear not, my dear; the armor of this carriage is thick and forged of the finest steel. No sword alone may hope to pierce its plating. We are stocked with enough provisions that our enemy should tire and abandon us before we need emerge. Should luck be by our side-"

But Emrasarie had ceased to listen. Her unclasped hand had instead found the hidden pocket sewn within a crease along her dress, and not a second later there flashed the deadly shimmer of a dagger let loose from its hold. The arcing path it took struck the eupatrid's neck with a splash of grisly red. Pressing harder still, she slid the weapon from ear to ear in a single stroke, and Aresh Lonnaskae, his eyes swollen in disbelief and fear, could do naught to hold back the blood now bursting free from the wound, drowning him in the very font of life that, only seconds before, had flowed securely through his body.

The deed done, Emrasarie sighed in relief. Though little joy was to be found in the act of killing, there was similarly no great amount of sorrow to dwell upon should the need arise. It was, after all, merely business, and as their continued survival remained ever tied to not only what they pilfered, but also the silence kept by those who had been pilfered from, Death proved an inescapable companion along many a past emprise shared.

Once the bloodstains were removed from her dagger, Emrasarie returned the weapon to the secret pocket in her dress. Her fingers brushed against the small glass vial the lining also shared, that receptacle in which was kept the venom she'd painted on her lips. Drawn and distilled into the malefic substance from vast quantities of rhogalida spider fangs, its slightest contact sank as if a slowly burning inferno into any soft and pulpous surface, and did so with a vehemence dependent upon the amount directly applied. Even the sparse layer she wore, atop a protective salve she'd smeared underneath to ward away its influence, had caused those areas the unsuspecting mercenaries were afflicted with to waste away into smoldering ruins of stringy and dripping viscera over the span of an hour or so, subjecting the sufferers to an agony from which there could be no respite.

Eager to be free of the danger its continued presence still presented, she dutifully wiped her lips with a spare cloth kept for just such a purpose. Throwing the stained rag aside, Emrasarie reached out across the corpse beside her for the latch sealing tight the carriage door. A single pull and it slid away, allowing her to finally swing the barrier open.

Waiting just beyond was a man ursine and towering in stature. Long dark hair fell past broad shoulders in a tempest of tangled strands, obscuring his face as if a cowl, and the platelets of the armored chest piece he wore made terrible the shadows cast at his feet. He carried with him a sword of monstrous immensity, and Emrasarie could see the thick sheen of blood glistening like starlight against its length. Fearful though his guise appeared, she smiled her true, untempered smile when, noticing his way now unbarred, the man strode with single-minded purpose towards her through the slaughter he had so effortlessly wrought, an equally relieved expression brightening the long and haggard lines of his face.

"The night is less dark being reunited once more," she cooed as Uralant scooped her in his arms. They embraced with a kiss, falling fully into one another, forgetting all the world around them. In that one moment, the only thing which mattered was their return to each other's side, and thoughts of riches and treasure and guarded spoils scattered into clouds of inconsequential fancy.

Yet always did those clouds eventually regather. Quickly did they return this time, blotting out any other thought from Emrasarie's mind, until the insatiable hunger to know what they had procured on this night remained all she could think of. Unable to bear it any longer, she thereby directed their attention back towards the carriage, and the lifeless occupant sprawled across its seat beneath a sheet of still glistening crimson.

"Did he hurt you?" asked Uralant, his voice resonating like gravel as he peered with contempt upon the eupatrid's pallid visage.

"Boredom was the only threat he posed me; boredom and no small amount of nausea. Though should his prize be equal to even half the boasts he made, I would gladly suffer another hour of such danger! Shall we?"

Climbing back into the carriage, Emrasarie regarded the blood-soaked Aresh Lonnaskae with all the disgust she had restrained during their brief time together. She tore loose from his chest a brooch of most curious hue, which she had eyed the moment entry into his company had been given. No doubt something of great personal worth and value, due to the prominence its placement had earned.

Though its beauty currently lay marred beneath such a grisly flood as had poured from its wearers throat, she nevertheless tossed the jewel to Uralant, unwilling to let anything of apparent value be left behind.

At last, she fell upon what had become the object of her desire. Expecting the case within the floor compartment to be burdensome, she was instead surprised to find it but a trifle in her arms as she lifted, lighter even than some tomes she had happened to carry in the past. She paused, marveling as to how something which carried such value to both the eupatrid and his potential buyer could be so light in her hands, before setting it on one of the carriage's empty chairs.

"What is it?" she heard Uralant behind her.

So great was her own excitement, so deeply had her mind fallen intoxicated into those tumultuous whirlpools of anticipation, she heeded not the whispers warning her towards suspicion as to why something so valuable had little more than a latch to safeguard it from unwelcome attention. Her only thought was to behold what their extensive planning, preparation, and subterfuge aimed towards this one target might at long last offer them. Grinning excitedly to Uralant, she wasted no further time, and threw the sealed case open.

Inside was but a tattered scrap of parchment. Held firm beneath a layer of glass casing, the sheet was gnarled to an ugly umber hue by the ravenous appetite of untold ages gone by. She caught a glimpse of text written across its face – symbols she could not read, but which were disquieting and unnatural, as if hinting at something purely malevolent in their design – before both they and the material on which they were transcribed then vanished, lost behind the glare of swelling sable light, while a strange heat began to sear against her face, as if the air itself had somehow caught aflame.

Emrasarie suddenly found herself hurtling through the air. With Uralant's iron grip wrapped around her, she fell away from the parchment and into a tumbling heap upon the ground afar. By the slightest breath had they escaped the maw of flames suddenly erupting from that case, an inferno which devoured in its ravenous teeth the entire structure of the carriage, along with everything it had once carried.

Shaken and left sprawled across the ground, the pair could only stumble back to their feet once too little fuel remained for the pyre to continue its feasting. Left behind was naught but acrid fumes sputtering in the charred and immolated air. They could just make out the panicked gallop of those horses which had drawn the carriage receding down the forest road, faint embers of still flaming harnesses billowing wildly in their wake.

What remained of the vehicle, meanwhile, smoldered in a burning ruin before them. It scarred the earth with a dark echo preternatural in its sensation, and left but fistfuls of ash for them to sift through in vain.

III

"STUPID, stupid, stupid!"

Uralant winced as Emrasarie severed the hush of early morning with her continued outbursts. She was still scowling when he glanced down at her, face pinched into a mask of sharply cut angles, while her eyes, narrowed to piercing thorns, stared at without truly observing the cityscape ahead.

They had finally reached the outskirts of Lucrauna after a grueling night navigating the long and precarious road. Cleaned of the soot, sweat, and blood that had darkened their already somber aspects, Uralant couldn't help but feel a slight rush of exhilaration to see the city at last spread before them.

Nestled in the cradle of a saucer-like vale, and spread out along the southern banks of the Amaranthyn's broad and gentle waters, he realized only now just how little they knew of what to expect here. The city lay deep in the isolated reaches of the Ingroliths, far and away from the coastal lands which formed the nexus of their known world. He recounted coming across its name at the Aphelaeum in Byrethlia, during his time as a neophyte scribe, where it had been interspersed within occasional lyrics of transcribed ballads it was his duty to organize, or buried amidst written avalanches of lengthy verse. Studiousness, however, had never been his guiding star, and further details he might have gleaned in those days were lost behind the ever-shrouding fog which follows time. They were entering such a place as remained unmarked in the maps his mind could draw upon, and despite the bleak circumstances by which they did, Uralant looked ahead ever eager as to what might be found in so alluring and august a place.

Returning his gaze to the road ahead, he nevertheless wished their arrival could have been upon the weightless wings following triumph, rather than the ball-and-chain slog trailing bitter defeat.

With tired steps did they traverse through the marmoreal avenues of the still-sleeping city. On every side were they flanked by expansive domiciles guarded by rows of great and towering columns, thrown to the sky so as to support the multiple levels of their construction, and crowned by sharply steepled rooves and chimney stalks still sputtering the last whispers of smoke from hearths within. The space between them, meanwhile, swam in the light of lanterns draped like vines along high cornices and overhead archways. Their multi-hued silk casings painted the city with brilliantly elusive tones spanning from one end of the rainbow to the other, and became entwined with those swirling fingers of mist spilling up from the Amaranthyn along the areas where streets and elevated walkways reached out across the river's placid current.

Silence as of a hushed breath held tight the air through which their aimless path led, a quiet more akin to a secret than the innocent lull of slumber, and though their way remained mostly emptied, Uralant noted those few souls they did pass were possessed of an airy, almost languid gait, shuffling away to unknown haunts with faces obscured by shadows of the pre-dawn gloom.

At length the pair paused along one of the waterway streets. There they leaned upon a balustrade supported by little caryatids caught in sensuous dance, and watched the river as it lapped against the channel walls below, bringing along helpless bits of flotsam to be carried off further downstream.

"I should have guessed!" she sighed, throwing back her head in exasperation as she toyed with the stolen brooch. "I should have known a eupatrid of Iskalruun would not be so lax in safe-guarding something he believed to be precious! But sorcery? How was I to suppose he would even have the means of utilizing those darkest arts in such a way, or the acumen to have that aim realized? And now, we have naught but this trinket to show for all our efforts!"

Uralant draped a hand atop her slender shoulder and squeezed just firmly enough to pull her back to the present moment. "We have each other still," he offered with a smile. "And who's to say the scrap of parchment you saw truly held what value the eupatrid claimed? Perhaps he was mistaken of its nature, or had deluded himself into believing it more than an ordinary sheaf cut from some ancient tome."

Doubt creased the edges of Emrasarie's eyes as she shook her head. "I think not. There was something...strange about that artifact. I wish you had chanced to see it; some aspect of its nature or the symbols scrawled upon it might have been recognizable. But now, it is gone forever, along with whatever worth it might have brought."

"More opportunities will present themselves. We need but be patient to see fortune swing back in our favor."

"Patience is a poor currency to subsist on, my love."

He was quiet then, and their shared silence was soon overwhelmed by the trickle of commotion following Lucrauna's waking. There was little he could say that would not ring hollow beside the singing clatter of bells struck at the peaks of temple towers, nor be trampled beneath the carts and over-stuffed wagons furiously searching out those best spots in markets squares and heavily-trafficked intersections. He had no words to offer as their wanderings through the city resumed, shared this time by crowds pouring out from the doors of their houses, and in whose steady meandering flow their own forms were soon lost.

But with their packs and pockets thoroughly emptied of funds, the weight of Emrasarie's word lingered upon his thoughts as they continued on. What still remained after that failure – namely the vial of rhogalida venom and a few final strands of necromantic twine – was doubtful to fetch any buyers in so idyllic and urbane a place as this. Even the brooch Emrasarie carried could not be guaranteed a reward of considerable, or even mediocre size. Their situation was truly dire, and Uralant did not have an answer as to how they might escape it.

Emrasarie, meanwhile, used the thronging ruck to her advantage. With deft fingers did she lift the occasional coin from unassuming autochthons, who suspected naught of a slight jostle from some pretty passerby, until they held enough to afford rudimentary lodgings at the first inn they came across. The matron within led them to an upstairs room furnished with but a bed, water basin, and chamber pot. Sparse though its furnishings were, Uralant counted himself lucky as any highborn liege, nestled beside a hearth in flowing furs, after the sleepless night they had endured amidst the mountain wilds, and so fell into the soft embrace of merciful slumber beside Emrasarie upon the mattress.

When next he stirred, it was to the deep ochre of a late-afternoon sun streaming into the room's only window, and the realization that the bed's other side lay vacant its previous occupant. A quick glance about the room confirmed he was alone, and from the coolness of the sheets where she had slept, he guessed Emrasarie had not been present for some time.

No doubt she had already departed to some market vendor or curio dealer with the eupatrid's brooch in hand, eager to ascertain what value it might bring them. Uralant let loose a heavy sigh as he heaved himself upright, blurry-eyed and aching throughout his thickly corded limbs. His stomach growled and, uncertain as to how long it might be before his beloved would return, he thought now as good a time as any to indulge in whatever victuals might be available here.

Forgoing armor, he dressed only in the dark tunic and trousers of his usual attire, feeling little need to encumber himself for something so simple as acquiring to a meal. He still carried with him to the inn's common room below his trusted blade, however, hesitant to be parted from the cold finality of its sacredly maintained edge. He let it rest flat upon the floor as he dropped to a mat in one of the small room's corners, and thanked the matron when she brought a plate of figs, quail eggs, and slightly-staled bread out to him.

"She is beautiful," the homely woman said, remaining by his side even as he began to eat. "The one you arrived with earlier today; truly beautiful."

Uralant grunted, uncertain what the matron aimed for or where this conversation might lead.

"She has come for the Frolic, no doubt. And none too soon! Tonight marks the final trip it will take down the Amaranthyn for the season. A lucky thing she arrived when she did. Fate seems to smile so often on some more than others, don't you think?"

When Uralant told her he had no knowledge of these things, her eyes widened in genuine surprise.

"You have not heard of the Frolic? Nor of Numynaris's Ark? Oh, forgive me. So often is it the case that when one such as she arrives, the Frolic is the sole object on their mind."

"She knows as little in this matter as me."

"Indeed," she nodded, though when she looked back at him, an odd expression filled the heavy lines of her face, as if she knew something he was woefully ignorant of. "Well, whatever the case, she would no doubt be granted entry should she come to desire such a thing."

Before she could further speak, other patrons of the inn - lovely and handsome patrons - drew the matron away, and left Uralant alone with his bristling thoughts.

A note of pity had been unmistakable in her voice; the same sanctimonious glib he had heard a hundred times over from a hundred different voices, each certain of Emrasarie's inner motives but by a single glance at her and all her readily flaunted radiance, in contrast to his own apparent dour and irascible demeanor. Jaw clenched and fingernails digging into his fist, Uralant nevertheless kept calm his composure. He knew naught would come of acting on the burning instinct coursing through his veins, and was loathe to succumb to the same reckless tendency for physical response as had proved so troublesome in the past.

He'd had so little control of himself back then. A 'monster,' the other neophytes had called him, both behind his back and spat at his face. In their hateful eyes, he had loomed brutish beyond even the capability of a lifetime of tutelage within the Aphelaeum to mend, liable to leave boys twice his age beaten to a bloody stupor by the happenstance of Fate having endowed him with a surplus of brawn to the detriment of brains. Of his scribe brothers' own cruelty towards him – the teasing and derision and torturous behavior proceeding his eventual fits of rage – the grand scholars remained blissfully ignorant. In their eagerness to return to the quiet sanctity of study, they had seen fit to remove the symptom of their problem rather than the cause, and so shut the doors to the House of Records behind Uralant, excising him to the vast and unforgiving city beyond without a coin to his name, or ally to stand watch when sleep stole what meager defenses his waking self was able to muster.

Though he managed on this occasion to remain level-headed, Uralant could not prevent his thoughts from tumbling down those shadowy corridors of suspicion regarding the aforementioned Frolic, and of how readily the matron had tied whatever its occurrence meant to his beloved.

Little time was afforded to ponder such things, however. Not several minutes later there entered through the building's door a trio of hard-visaged men, adorned in heavy coats of leather and swords swinging ominously from their belts.

Uralant immediately knew danger followed in their wake. His keen eyes had witnessed enough of its varying shades to know when violence was imminent, dark as a thunderstorm on the horizon. Taking the hilt of his own sword in hand, he had drawn its length across his lap by the time the interlopers' scowls fell upon him. In short succession they then crossed the room, encircling him as they did so, glowering with menace and threatening posture.

"You are Uralant the Untamable, are you not?" the center-most figure asked with brusque insistence.

"And if I am?"

"Then we bid you follow us at once."

"You have given neither your names, your purpose, nor your intentions, and yet wish for me to follow blindly at your beck and call?"

The man who had spoken narrowed further his eyes. "You need none of those to know you are outmatched, and thereby beholden to our demands."

Each of the three placed hands on the hilts of their swords.

"Is that so?" stated Uralant, the weight of his own weapon disappearing into the grip of a tightly-clenched fist.

"Should you refuse, then our master cannot guarantee the continued safety of Emrasarie."

For the briefest moment, all hold of himself vanished from Uralant's mind. There was only his rage, the fiery-eyed beast slumbering ever inside his heart, which would consume him entirely in its burning ire were he to allow it to do so.

"Oh ho, that got his attention!" the man to his right cackled. "You heard right; we've got your little hetaera, kept where she can't cause any more trouble. Such a pretty thing too!"

The rage reared greater still, threatening to burst clear through the bulging sinews spread across Uralant's body. "You seek my compliance, yes?" he growled quietly, meeting each of his enemy's eyes in turn as he spoke. "Tell me; you named me as 'the Untamable.' Quite the moniker, no? In light of that, and similar knowledge you must then also possess, answer me this: do you believe yourselves to be the ones to finally tame me?"

Almost faster than the eye could follow did his sword fly through the air. With a dark slash it swept out to meet the calves belonging to the man at his right. Immediately was the self-assured sneer, so dominant upon his face mere seconds ago, stolen by a pallor of panicked confusion, then a cry as agony finally tore through his senses. The man collapsed atop the bloody stumps left at the ends of each leg, there no longer being any feet attached to stand upon, his previous mirth obliterated by the howling screams let loose as he flailed helplessly across the floor.

The other two reeled back in shock, fumbling to fully draw their weapons while Uralant lunged forward from the floor. He collided into the man to his left, bringing them both to a heap on the ground. Sprawled astride his winded enemy, there flashed the deadly shimmer of swinging steel along Uralant's periphery, and he just barely raised his own weapon in time to parry an attempted blow from the middle figure.

Shocked by the fortitude of that unexpected defense, his attacker was caught unawares as Uralant then lashed out with his freed hand, grasping the upright man's ankle and pulling his weight out from under him. He fell hard to the floor, and the next instant was the shadow of Uralant's mighty sword brought overhead. Its point skewered down like the deadly spike atop a unicorn's brow, puncturing clear through thick leather and drenching the man's chest in a pool of seething crimson.

"Have mercy, please!" gasped the one still lying beneath him. "We didn't hurt her, I swear! Our orders were only-"

Without so much as a hesitating glance did Uralant clasp a hand on each side of the pleading man's head. He then twisted with the vicious force of his full and unrepentant strength, and the sharp snapping of the man's neck tore through the room like a culminating note to the gruesomely orchestrated ballad in which they had been engaged.

Lurching to his feet, he made across the room as if a man spurred by the solemn horns of war, ignoring the dumb-founded faces too cowardly or frightened to lift even a passing hand in aide. His only thought was of slamming through the door and finding Emrasarie, wherever she might have been taken. He would overturn every stone and break through every threshold within the city should he need to, the roaring beast that was his rage spurring him blindly ahead into Lucrauna's streets.

He was thereby caught off-guard when, upon stepping outside, there waited an even larger retinue of armed men upon the road, no less than a dozen strong, their weapons already drawn and leveled his way.

"So good of you to finally join us, Uralant," a figure at the rear of their formation spoke, clapping with obvious glee as he approached.

Frocked in black albs draped down his tall form like ink cascading from an overturned stopper, the man wore upon his face a mask of flawless and ornately formed silver, its perimeter surrounded by long extrusions flaring out from the center. The features there were cut into the sharply defined angles of a leering, wickedly-cherubic smile, and seeing his own reflection twisted and made gruesome in that mirror-like surface, Uralant shivered, realizing only then his rage, which had burned so bright only a moment ago, was quelled to ashes by fear's frozen touch. He knew he had no choice but to throw down his sword in defeat. His strength, after all, would count for precious little when come face to face with a sorcerer such as this, one who hailed, as was evident by the severe aspect of his mask, from the very seat of power which the eupatrid slain the previous night had similarly called home.

"A wise decision indeed!" the sorcerer of Iskalruun laughed as the abandoned blade clattered against the paved roadside, and directed his hired hands to bind Uralant. "Yes, there may yet be some use for you! Now come; we wouldn't want to keep dear Emrasarie waiting, would we?"

IV

EMRASARIE slumped low upon the settee to which she was bound. The manacles around her wrists had already begun to leave ugly welts along the skin there, punishment for the wholly ineffectual straining she had attempted against them earlier. Though externally she rested, within her mind forged relentlessly ahead in search for some secret avenue by which she might find an escape, some heretofore unnoticed aspect of the room she could use to her advantage.

Every potential pathway she envisioned quickly vanished under the faintest light of scrutiny. Even if she somehow managed to free herself from the heavy iron holds and flee the chamber to which she had been brought, its only door remained guarded by two powerfully-built men holding spears at attention, while the wide balcony looking out across Lucrauna opposite them led nowhere but a fifty-meter freefall to the ground below.

The tower in which she had been imprisoned rose as a grand affair of soaring stone above the rooftops of Lucrauna. Whether it had been acquired for her current captors by legitimate means, or through more forceful persuasion, she could not say, though it certainly lacked none of the fine trappings she had so intimately known while still in the business of entertaining the powerful and prosperous of Byrethlia. Mercifully, none of the sell-swords who'd whisked her away from the market streets below had entered the room once she was secured by lock and chain. Though her head swam with countless questions as to the reasons for her capture, Emrasarie was thankful she had yet to contend with the possibility of interrogation, or worse, torture, especially should it come from the horrid man at their lead, the one who wore the smiling silver mask.

She had thought herself in a nightmare when that vizard emerged from the crowds, with its warped attempts to hint at a serene and perfectly flawless expression. The desire to imitate all the most pleasing aspects of a face had, however, resulted in something closer to a grotesquerie, and she had nearly shrieked as the figure swept forward, snatching from her hands the eupatrid's brooch she'd had outstretched towards a vendor's discerning eye. The crown framing the mask's upper half jutted out like the barbs of some monstrous breed of cactus waiting to pierce any fool who dared draw too close, and it had flashed dangerously in the sunlight so close to her. Worse still, there had then slithered through the grinning lips a cold and haunting voice that spoke her name, breathing out its disparate syllables with such suffocating intimacy her skin still crawled at the recollection.

What so loathsome a fiend wanted of her, or how he knew without introduction or provocation the truth of her identity, were questions Emrasarie feared to find answers for.

The manacle chains cackled at her attempts to thrash against them once again. And again her efforts rang out in vain. As minutes dragged by, and the sky beyond bruised to darker and deeper shades of violet, she dreaded to guess what Uralant must be thinking now. Surely it had been hours since he'd noticed her gone, and without any knowledge of where she might be, what fears must his mind have conjured to explain so sudden and lengthy a disappearance?

A bolt of despair struck her then. The thought she might forever be separated from her beloved suddenly cut through all other consideration, and the wound it left festered darker than any night of odious venery she'd ever been forced to endure, bringing to her eyes the scalding shimmer of tears.

Emrasarie scrunched her face in denial to such a prospect. Uralant would find her. He had to. They always found one another, ever since the disparate strings of their fates had been entwined within the depths of Byrethlia's most despicable slums. There they had found the strength within each other to survive against so many cruel odds set against them. Only together had they crawled free from the dregs of that despair, before Death could claim either of them for itself. Only together had hope seemed a possibility worth striving for. She knew he would not give up now. And she could not lose faith in him.

Heavy footsteps from the adjoining stairs dispelled like a dream the bleak reverie into which Emrasarie had fallen. Forcing her eyes into cold and sharpened points, she made ready to face her captors with newfound and hardened insolence, prepared to snarl and spit and spew curses at the sorcerer and his dreadfully silvered visage.

She was thereby taken aback when it was the hulking outline of her beloved brought in through the doorway, weaponless and held in restraints similar to her own.

"Uralant!" she gasped.

Shoved into the room by his captors, Uralant's eyes widened to see her there. He hurried over to where she sat and dropped to his knee beside her, taking as best he could her bound hands in his.

"I feared the worst when they told me you were taken," he said, shaking his head. "I was so worried I had failed you, and knew not what I would do were you harmed in any way."

Smiling despite the severity of their situation, Emrasarie shook her head, wishing desperately she could have reached high enough to soothe the bristling concern flushing Uralant's cheek a dangerous crimson. "You have not failed, my love. You are here, and I am safe."

"But what is the cause of all this? What business have these cut-throats and their sorcerous master with us?"

"You humble yourself, mighty Uralant!" a shrill and muffled voice suddenly pierced from the direction her beloved had come. "It is the very business you and Emrasarie so indulge that has brought our paths together on this fortuitous evening. Oh yes, your reputations are well known to me. Brigands of your type, no matter how thorough or careful you may attempt to remain, are never so invisible as you no doubt believe yourselves to be."

The sorcerer swept into the room like smoke billowing up from a freshly-stoked fire. For a moment he simply stood there, the flowing contours of his mask trapping the candlelight cast upon its surface as if a mirror, one which warped and twisted the glistening ribbons of luminescence into horribly evocative shapes. Even the sell-swords in his service seemed nervous in sharing the same space as him. Whether aware of this or not, the sorcerer then signaled his company to leave, so the three of them were left as the room's sole occupants.

Somehow, their departure only made the artificial face which gleamed opposite them even more unsettling to behold.

"What is it you want from us, sorcerer?" bellowed Uralant.

"I would have your lives for what your actions cost me, and how severely they have set my aims back."

"We are innocent of whatever it is you claim!" snapped Emrasarie. "Whatever loss you have suffered lays upon someone else's hands, not ours!"

"Oh? Then perhaps you might tell me how this came to be in your possession?" The brooch she had taken from Aresh Lonnaskae suddenly appeared in the sorcerer's outstretched hand, its polished surface glinting in the dim light like an unpleasant memory which steals sleep from a tired mind. "One does not often find a commoner trapsing about openly with a heraldic badge belonging to one of Iskalruun's eupatridae in hand. The markings here denote it as House Lonnaskae, I do believe, which means this should be pinned upon the chest of their current patriarch, Aresh Lonnaskae. Curious, though, I should have spied it with you, and not him."

"We met Lonnaskae the previous night, its true!" Emrasarie blurted in rising panic. "But it was only as fellow travelers along the road. He must have taken pity on us and our sorry state, for he offered the brooch to us so it might be used to acquire shelter and supplies wherever we next happened upon. Any misfortune befallen him after we parted ways is unknown to us!"

An audible scoff slipped through the sorcerer's mask. "My, my; who knew old Aresh had such magnanimity hidden away in his heart! Perhaps he will be more accommodating to my own wishes as well! You see, I have a certain interest in finding our wayward eupatrid. He fled from glorious Iskalruun a month's span past, ferrying with him a treasure which her Resplendency, the Queen Empyreal, desperately wished to procure. I ascertained his path would lead him to these distant lands, and was to lie in wait for his eventual arrival, ready to convince through whatever means necessary that its relinquishment unto me would be far preferable to whatever sum of gold his newfound buyer might have promised. And yet, I have spied not a single trace of him. No ostentatious carriage; no procession of armed mercenaries; only this little brooch, carried in your lovely, no doubt blood-stained hands."

Emrasarie glowered at their captor, cursing herself for having taken the damned brooch in the first place, though this time remained silent. The sorcerer, meanwhile, seemed to bask in his own mordancy, the smoothed and intricately-carved facets of his mask causing the reflected candlelight to quiver as if in silent laughter.

"Oh, but you must forgive me," he continued. "I've neglected to share what some of my hired swords reported earlier. It seems the charred remains of a carriage, one of Iskalruun make and build, was found on the western road leading from Lucrauna. With it were the carcasses of men cut down by what must have been a truly monstrous sword, while their faces were succumb to the ghastly effects of rhogalida venom. Alas, I fear the chance to reconvene and procure what I sought from the little fool has been denied to me."

"What do you intend to do then, if you are so certain of our guilt?" Uralant barked.

For a moment the sorcerer only stared, any hint of contemplation masked behind the frozen face he wore. At length he turned from them, sauntering to the balcony so as to look out across the city afar, and Emrasarie, no longer forced to endure so malicious and arrogant an expression, let free a secret breath of relief.

A stream of words then spewed from the sorcerer's direction. Sounds of no tongue she recognized, and which rang loathsome and guttural in their proclamation, as if such phrases should have never been explicated from the lacking lips of men. Suddenly were the shackles binding her and Uralant broken of their previously steadfast grips, and the heavy iron links fell uselessly upon the floor.

Blinking at the unforeseen occurrence, Emrasarie, touched gingerly at the red marks left on her flesh, as if to make certain the source from which her lingering pain stemmed was truly gone. Beside her, Uralant rose to the full immensity of his height. She could see the fury unleashed within his eyes, squared directly at the exposed back of their enemy, and the precarious ledge upon which he stood.

She grabbed hold of her beloved's arm, holding tight so as to prevent any brash or misguided decision he might have made. The fire softened then, and he returned to her a somber look as he helped her to her feet.

"My only desire," said the sorcerer, "is to see the will of my Queen done. And I may not return to her audience until what she has entrusted me to acquire finally rests in my hands. You, Uralant and Emrasarie, have waylaid me in my ultimate triumph. Yet while the treasure Aresh Lonnaskae unwittingly had passed down into his unworthy hands was rare and valuable above all else to my Queen, it is not the only one of its kind. Many besides her Resplendency seek to gather such artifacts to their person, and it would appear the buyer to whom Aresh Lonnaskae sought recompense from was indeed one of these collectors, hungry to add yet another to their trove."

He then turned back to them and pointed: "Tell me; what have you heard of Numynaris's Ark?"

Emrasarie glanced again to Uralant. Though neither said a word, she could see the flicker of recognition dancing in his eyes, and so knew he had also now come across that same name, while remaining as equally oblivious to its significance as her.

"I thought not. Even the ears of her Resplendency the Queen Empyreal remained unaware of its existence afore these past few days. Well, you will then share in the surprise I too felt upon seeing it the first time."

The sorcerer beckoned them to join him on the balcony. Though her skin crawled to do so, Emrasarie obeyed, with Uralant following close as a shadow behind.

From so high a perch, the seemingly limitless lanterns of Lucrauna were spread like stars captured within the capricious and dazzling surface of an opal. Each street shone as bright as the one proceeding it, their varied colors coruscating together until the whole city flared as if a beacon within the vale, a solitary spark of civilization warding back the black waves of encroaching wilderness beyond. They were close to the Amaranthyn here, two or three avenues at most, and looking that way, Emrasarie marveled at the sheer breadth the river had swelled to at this junction. From shore to shore it reached such a distance so as to resemble more an idle lake than a coursing river, and its waters were carpeted by great swirling strokes of lotus blossoms. Their petals had been stained to purple beneath those lights cast by the lunar triune emerged in full overhead, and in places the colubrine current shimmered as if a ribbon of fine, vibrantly fuscous silk draped out across the earth.

That luster, however, was slowly beginning to fade. A heavy wall of mist poured across the river from further upstream, and submerged beneath it the violet currents flowing so slowly by. Uncertain as to what could cause such a phenomenon, Emrasarie suddenly spied something within the distant plumes of rolling vapor; a faint, yet tangible shape drifting in tow with the obscuring clouds that so thoroughly enveloped it. As if trepidatious to fully reveal itself yet, the object crawled with sluggish insistence ahead until, drawing abreast Lucrauna and its many riverside streets, it tore through the clinging veil and revealed itself in full.

"Beautiful, is it not?" the sorcerer mused beside her.

She had no words to answer. Her breath failed, stolen by that strangest of sensations, when awe and uneasiness throw themselves against one another in terrifying clamor. Attempting to make sense of the structure, and the monstrous vessel it sprawled atop, she found herself returned to past conversations at the pillow with clients fanatically devoted to the hidden language behind aesthetics and the nature of beauty, particularly in regards to its relationship with artifice.

Among poets, philosophers, and statesmen of deftly-honed rhetoric, the prevailing thought had gone that no matter how great mankind's conceit grew against the earthen cradle from which he'd first arisen, ever was there the desire to replicate in his own wonders the same sublime effortlessness seen throughout the natural world. So as a flower bursts into brilliance from a mere seed without exterior aide, so then would a sculptor, painter, or architect also wish their creation to appear as an act of sheer and unrestrained spontaneity, rather than the result of hands laboring at the behest of ponderous intent. Simplicity sat ever entwined with elegance upon the pedestal erected by those sharp-eyed aesthetes, and to deviate from that path, set out by the grand tapestry of existence connecting all things together, was to court disaster.

This feat of creation, and the way it erupted from the lotus-choked waters as if a fountain of flawlessly wrought, iridescent steel, seemed instead a complete and flagrant repudiation of such thinking. Somewhere within stupendously sheer walls and angles cut into one another with painfully rigid abruptness, Emrasarie recognized what appeared to be an amphitheater in intent. Its interior remained sealed away behind discordant aspects of construction and daunting geometric theorems, their individual facets holding firm a totality unable to have been conceived by anything other than the willful hubris of man. Its highest points pierced the sky in vaunted spires dizzying in their attempts to follow, while along the perimeter were spread supporting arcs soaring past the point of functional belief. Emrasarie could not imagine the minds able to envision what her own eyes struggled to comprehend, nor believe the sheer ingenuity needed to fit all its pieces together.

It was not, she dreaded to surmise, the shadow of men merely drunk on vanity that lurked at the heart of this thing's design. Only as a result of deranged and maniac autolatry could such a construct have been born; that complete severance of the soul from earthly surroundings, after which fires stoked of disgust seek to expel its bearers from the self-consuming coil which remains the world and dwell, instead, unencumbered in deific splendor from on high.

"That is a relic of Vyrkylos," muttered Uralant, giving name to the dread citadel said to have held supremacy across the sky itself in eons past.

"A learned man! Excellent; I was loathe to think your usefulness might only be as an unwieldy club, and not the scalpel I am in need of."

"But how can such a thing still be? Knowledge of that kind has long since faded from the world, has it not?"

"Faded, but not forgotten in full. Fragments of their power and wisdom linger even now. It is surely through the possession of one such fragment we may behold this pale shadow of what its original splendor once cast across the world. If the word of Lucrauna's wistful and starry-eyed denizens are to be believed, then there flourishes as well within its walls a glimpse of those eldren days amidst the clouds. A dedication to indulgence on nights such as these, when Merexiol, Amascryl, and Ilophrin frolic together on high, all orchestrated and maintained at the pleasure of a most enigmatic host."

From where they stood, Emrasarie saw tightly packed crowds scurrying below. They flooded the riverside streets and docks closest to the Ark like ants drawn to the remnants of discarded, over-ripe fruit, thronging against one another to get nearer the revealed structure in the river.

Despite the shock that had initially gripped her, Emrasarie found herself similarly unable to break free of the maliciously abstruse grandeur of the thing. It was as if her eyes had been speared by the same sharpness that stole the warring moonlights from atop the firmament, luminous echoes of vermillion, azure, and argent trickling like blood down high-flung turrets and plunging buttresses beyond count. A desire she could not name, a yearning she was afraid to speak aloud, reared itself awake within her then, and it was only by the sorcerer's continued speech she remained cognizant of the present moment.

"I aim to pilfer the Vyrkylian records certain to be in Numynaris's possession on this night. To do so, I require dishonorable and scheming brigands as yourselves to see my plans through. In recompense for the trouble you have seen fit to cause, the two of you will assist me in boarding the Ark and finding my rightful prize within."

Emrasarie shivered, though whether from nerves or anticipation, she could not say. Uralant, meanwhile, grunted in dismay, though said naught to the contrary.

Mind already racing, she noticed the Ark had come to a halt afar from Lucrauna's shoreline, either unwilling or unable to be moored to any of the extended platforms and quays jutting out like the assembled spears of an army into the Amaranthyn.

"But how would we even gain entry to such a place?" she asked.

Before she or Uralant could react, the sorcerer's hand extended in a shadowy flash and grabbed hold of Emrasarie's cheeks. He then pulled her so she could do naught else but stare into the twin voids of blackness that were his eyes.

"You will find, dear Emrasarie, our soon-to-be host has all but left the door ajar in anticipation for someone like you."

V

URALANT knew well the patience required in waiting for the precise moment a plan necessitate he act. He had endured such periods many a night before this, vital in so many of the schemes orchestrated between him and his beloved, and had always counted as familiar the toll its ordeal inevitably took.

Any familiarity to be found was absent this occasion, however, subsumed beneath the chagrin of sharing so many of those long and creeping minutes with one who, at the slightest whim, might determine his usefulness spent, and so surcease his life without a moment's pause.

He waited but a stone's throw from Zelaeus – the sobriquet given for their benefit by the sorcerer – on an ill-maintained, altogether abandoned dock, staring out across the Amaranthyn as a faint wind brushed at the wild strands of his hair and ruffled the long cloak he wore. Returned to his side was the comforting weight of his sword, and though its steel might have offered him some semblance of assurance any other time, tonight it only added to the strain he was forced to endure.

The added burden had been placed upon him by the sorcerer before they'd ventured out from the tower and towards the task at hand. At first glance, it appeared as if extravagant armor; a cuirass of cumbrous appearance, strangely segmented along the chest and with a humped protrusion sticking out from the back. Zelaeus had called it an arachyne, and whence brought into the room on a litter by two servants, it had conjured in Uralant's mind impressions of a steel-wrought crab or gigantic myriapod laid out upon its back, the many-jointed legs splayed outwardly from a curved body long and triangular in design.

At a few words from Zelaeus – words with the same horribly discordant aspect as those which had undone without need of lock or key the chains binding his hands – the thing had stirred, given life where before it had been inert. Long appendages had writhed with insidious intent, as if desperate to devour whatever prey the thing feasted upon, and no time was wasted by the servants in heaving up the arachyne and thrusting its underside against Uralant's back. The legs had snapped shut the moment they came into contact, sealing around him like a heavy carapace of steel, and from the severity inherent in its grip, liable to crush his body should it further tighten, there was needed no explanation as to the purpose behind this foul instrument.

Swatting his own discomforts aside, Uralant kept his gaze fixed upon the shoreline upstream, where the crowds buzzed and thronged in excited commotion along those areas closest to where the Ark had moored. Though he and the sorcerer had purposefully positioned themselves a sizeable distance from the scene, it and all its minute details were captured in full clarity by means of the scrying eye Zelaeus had conjured.

When held aloft towards what one wished to observe, the little ball of swirling incarnadine magnified in its dark and glowing depths what otherwise would have been indiscernible from so great a scope, and so now brought into crystalline focus not only those many faces waiting about the docks, but also the gondolas drifting through the water towards them. Their purpose, so it seemed, was to ferry unto the Ark individuals who were selected for admittance within the Frolic. This they performed with hurried insistence, maneuvered by figures all but shapeless beneath shrouds wrapped about them like loose-fitting cerements, and who stabbed their long oars into the languid water in what was little more than a mindless imitation of rowing.

Contrary to what he might have suspected, Uralant noticed those selected by the mute rowers and their oddly staccato gestures were not solely of wealth or societal rank; artisans, laborers, even those in the plain and rough-spun attire of fieldworkers, all seemed equally worth consideration for whatever waited out there on the river. While the exact reasoning behind each attendee chosen remained known only to the cloaked boatsmen, and presumably the master who had issued such a standard in the first place, it quickly became clear at least one unifying aspect was shared between each of the beaming faces allowed access to the Ark: beauty.

Not a single passenger enroute to the larger vessel afar would fail in stirring to a fiery blaze even the most dampened passions of one otherwise bound by stringently enforced vows of celibacy. The myriad women, some pert in their demeanor, others sublime as if carven of polished stone, sent Uralant's heart aflutter with primal yearning, while the men, chiseled and proud of feature, overwhelmed him with such sharp pangs of jealousy he could hardly bare to look upon them. As he scoured their procession trickling away from the shore, unable to tear his gaze away, the matron's words spoken earlier that same day came back to him, along with her prediction towards Emrasarie's inclusion in the Frolic.

Sure enough, the stir then caused by her appearance was palpable even without use of the scrying eye.

The masses parted like clouds breaking after the darkness of a storm. Uralant watched with bated breath as Emrasarie emerged there along the docks, poised as an icon cut from flawless ivory and wreathed within the sensuous comber of silken cerulean tides. A sharp pressure seized at his heart when one of the gondolas immediately drew close to where she stood. His throat tightened when she obeyed the motion given for her to board, taking the seat offered with graceful repose. As her presence dwindled away, consumed by the shadows fallen from the mock-Vyrkylian spectacle lurking beyond, a frore whisper ran the length of his spine, and he shivered despite the rage burning like magma through his veins.

Another bout of waiting now commenced with Emrasarie's ingress upon the Ark. Soon was Uralant reduced to pacing back and forth along the dock, throwing nervous looks towards the arcane structure as rotted planks creaked beneath his feet. Madness must have claimed him, he thought, to have abided in this aspect of the sorcerer's scheme.

It still baffled him, standing so close to something which had, until a few hours prior, always seemed closer to the realm of myth than tangible historical record. He had come across but few references to that citadel called Vyrkylos while sifting through the Aphelaeum's sprawling bookshelves and organizing the dust-riddled denizens therein, yet those sparse encounters had still managed to cast frightening shadows in their wake.

They recounted a society more akin to the fanatical dreams of augurs, whose visions had delved too deep into the yawning emptiness between stars on moonless nights, than a civilization ordered under the limits of human flesh and blood. Dark litanies were recited of a decadence which had been allowed to flourish to the furthest reaches of the firmament. The roaring appetite at its heart, fueled by butchery as left the very air weeping with gore, had sent the walls which housed its purveyors soaring as if upon the backs of gryphons into nubivigant splendor on high, lacking limit or ceiling to curtail their assent. Legends said Fate itself had grown jealous of the citadel's rule, however. Wings once capable of reaching to such supernal heights eventually withered black beneath the sun, and once the sky was stolen out from under them, those masters and all the blood-soaked wonder they had wrought could but plunge back down upon the lands below in a razing phlegethon of ruin.

Yet here, against all odds, floated a replica to that monument in miniature; as perfect an echo to its antephlegethontal memory as one could manage while still shackled to so mundane a surface as the world.

And they were meant to steal from the personage who had conceived to bring such a monstrosity back into being?

Naturally, both he and Emrasarie had inquired as to what was known regarding Numynaris, and the Frolic they were meant to smuggle themselves within, but Zelaeus had been disconcertingly ignorant towards such information. He had told them precise recollections of time aboard the Ark, and of the host who sought the company of those passion-stirring crowds they'd glimpsed, seemed not to follow the participants back to Lucrauna's shore. Some aspect of the occasion stole from them all but the most rudimentary impressions of lingering bliss, so that when returned to the docks where they'd previously boarded in the waning hours before dawn, the only certainty carried was that they had enjoyed such wild and unrestrained debauchery as stood without equal outside those walls.

Uralant remembered the wanderers they'd encountered upon arriving in the city not a full day past, and wondered whether the same fugue had so addled their steps, returned so recently from the Frolic and all its hinted delights. Unbidden to his mind now came glimpses of the carousing he imagined necessary to induce the stuporous state described; of feasting and drinking and singing with abandon through those great gulfs of the midnight realm, until merriment inevitably descended into a blazing whirlwind spun by abasements of eager flesh, culminating in such a cacophonous cry of ecstasy that the sun itself might hesitate its ascent the following morn, ashamed to illuminate the remnants of what had been performed outside its purview.

The idea of Emrasarie included in a bacchanal of that sort, utterly at the mercy of whomever lurked behind the eponym Numynaris and the whims of their surely salacious intent, ran like quicksilver through the endlessly branching caverns of his consciousness. It thereupon flooded every formation of thought under caustic waves bristling with apprehension and anger alike, and no matter how insistent his pacing grew, he found himself unable to escape its mire.

"What concerns you so, Uralant?" a sibilant whisper crept suddenly into his ears.

Reeling about, Uralant balked to see the sorcerer not a forearm's lengths away, the mask so close its haughty leer gobbled up his shocked expression in full and threw the warped reflection back at him with repulsive clarity. Had he not known the thing to be forged of burnished silver, Uralant would have sworn its smile curled wider and with a more wicked bent than it had before.

"Surely you have faith in your Emrasarie, and the task she has been set on?" Zelaeus continued. "How lovely she shone, after all, even amidst so many other treasures there along the shore."

Turning away, Uralant cursed this fiend who currently plagued him, thinking only of maintaining his watch on the Vyrkylian spires afar.

"Ah, but perhaps it is not faith you lack. Perhaps you fear what will happen should Emrasarie join so lofty a company as gathered within the Ark, and finds she enjoys their presence far more than she ever did yours."

"Be silent!" Uralant growled, stomping further down the dock. "You know not of what you speak."

"But I do know exquisiteness when I see it, and what becomes of such luster when it is prevented from shining as it truly wishes. It strikes me that Emrasarie is one who wishes to dazzle like a diamond set within a diadem, one fit for an empress no less. Yet here must she resign herself, remaining dull and commonplace while ever shackled to your side. I wonder, then, how brightly she will shine in the confines of the Frolic, and if, given the choice afterwards, she would even return here at all?"

Rage sank its claws into his legs and dragged Uralant to a violent stop. He turned back at the sorcerer, his vision bathed in furious red, and instinctually raised a hand to the hilt of his sword. One swing was all he needed; one strike and his enemy would be no more.

"Careful, my friend," Zelaeus warned, motionless as a statue, his voice sickeningly calm. "Your blade may be swift, but I assure you my words are quicker still. I will not hesitate in sacrificing the strength you might have otherwise provided should you prove more liability than asset. And should you be slain, then Emrasarie's own usefulness will be spent once she fulfills her present role. Who then will see to it she finds her way from the Frolic's clutches, once my business aboard is concluded?"

They faced opposite each other in silence, neither willing to break their stance. Only the faint muttering of a gentle breeze, interspersed by little waves lapping against the gnarled piles rising up from the water below, disturbed their stalemate. Then, just as Uralant had steeled himself for the worst, something in the distance caught the sorcerer's attention.

"Ah! what fortuitous timing!" he cackled.

Wary of some trick being played upon him, Uralant waited until it was apparent Zelaeus's gaze was wholly stolen by whatever it was he'd seen, and only then followed where his gesture had pointed out across the river. There, along the Ark's tapered bow, he caught a faint glimpse of something not present a moment before. It was, as the scrying eye showed, a long strand of rope, the same one which Emrasarie had concealed by the use of strategic knots and coils beneath her dress. Just as the sorcerer's plan dictated, it now dangled all the way from the deck otherwise unreachable to any excluded parties down to the Amaranthyn's placid face. The orbiting gondolas did not, in their repeated paths to and from the crowded shores, come so far up the vessel's length to risk happening upon its placement, and though the chord swayed fully in the open for any wandering eye to see, so innocuous a detail would no doubt be obliterated from any passing glance, unable to contend with the sheer ostentation that overflowed from the obvolute and gargantuan spectacle above.

"We must be off," Zelaeus announced, and made towards a small coracle moored along the dock, left there from earlier that same evening. "Or, should you prefer, I can send you to a bloody slumber beneath these waters."

It was with a heavy and reluctant sigh Uralant at last released his grip from his sword hilt. He boarded the craft behind the sorcerer without a word, his fury towards the masked fiend tempered only by his unwillingness to leave Emrasarie alone with so dark a burden were his body to be broken and cast aside into the cold depths of Oblivion.

They pushed free from the dock once both were seated, and Uralant, guiding them ahead by powerful strokes of the oar, watched as Zelaeus drew forth great vaporous clouds from the previously emptied air through more foul and sorcerous words, obscuring their progress from the notice of any curious eyes on the shores afar.

VI

SHE was losing herself; with every drawn out and sumptuous second, Emrasarie could feel her very sense of self slipping out from between her fingers.

Into silken blades of grass bursting like emerald fountains through their gaps. Into earth unblemished by rock or stone obtrusions, its softness closer to a bed against her back than the rolling slope of a hillock. Into air that was a dream to imbue, warm enough to leave exposed flesh glistening beneath a faint and all-together tantalizing glow, and which carried wisps of freshly burned incense in its depths, sweet and sensuous and stifling.

Why would she ever wish to pull herself free?

This could not still be the amphitheater upon the Ark she'd entered, could it? Forcing her eyes open, she squinted at the strange erubescent light which greeted her, and craned her head up from the prone position she had been laying.

There spread the broad expanse of a garden all around her, lawns dotted here and there with luxuriant trees bursting from the supple earth, perennials and poppy plants exploding in vibrant colors at their roots. No walls could be seen bordering the area, nor opened portals through which she might have come, just an encircling and nacreous veil, billowing like some vast spectral stampede swept up in the distant reaches beyond. So thoroughly had this place been swaddled by the eclipsing wall of their procession that a potent, wholly captivating sensation of kalopsia had sunk its ravenous fangs into her mind. It gorged without repentance upon the dim recollections of any life she'd previously possessed, that time deemed wholly inconsequential now, until naught aside these idyllic environs and the pleasures offered therein seemed worth her regard any longer.

Why would she bother remembering anything else?

Encumbered as if recently submerged in water, Emrasarie let her head fall back to the cool grass below. Overhead, there blazed a starfield of scintillating embers across a sealed and vaulted sky, showering upon her so deep a radiance she found herself unable to look away, unable to conceive that there might be another firmament outside. Their pallor drenched the quiet air, and drenched deeper still herself, leaving her drowned beneath the same titian glow which cascades from stained glass at the sunset hour, ready to stir the heart aflame and unleash such desire as remains all but forbidden under daylight's harsh and scolding glare.

As if summoned by those yearnings, Emrasarie felt a hand graze across her cheek. She instinctively leaned towards its touch, her heart pounding, before alighting her gaze with the bearer of that hand. If there was a face she had been expecting, the woman's she beheld, round and framed by thick locks of tussled auburn, was not it. Laid close beside her, there existed only pruriency in the lovely contours which she boasted, accentuated by the warm effulgence washed over what little clothes she still wore, and those thick shadows straining to cover what was no longer concealed. Without speaking a single word, there passed between them the woman's unquenchable need to hold, to feel, to embrace another's flesh, along with the expectancy such sentiments be reciprocated unto her.

At a loss as to what was happening or who this woman was, Emrasarie realized another hand had descended, this one taking her palm in a powerful grip. She knew before she looked this belonged to a man, one revealed to be every bit as impressive and handsome as the woman was comely and fair. The same insatiable and hedonic appetite filled his smiling face, just as it had the woman's, and when he then leaned forward, he kissed at the underside of her wrist with a delicacy as of one who has come upon a treasure more precious than even the most flawlessly cut gemstone hewn from the world's riven heart.

Emrasarie did not immediately move to rebuke them. They were, after all, each so beautiful; beautiful and captivating and enticing, the same as everything else in this place. Was there aught else that mattered? a soft, horribly tantalizing voice asked from somewhere deeper than her ears. What greater pleasure could be had than to indulge in this beauty offered to her, and in turn offer herself up to it?

The blinding thrall of passion had nearly overwhelmed her when there came to Emrasarie the recollection of another face. She paused, taken aback by its sudden intrusion within her mind. Compared to her present company, this internal visage lacked in almost every quality to be found, and she knew were its presence to have manifested before them, it would be abhorred without mercy by all those engaged in this Frolic. The voice nibbling beneath her flesh warned her to turn away; to ignore this untoward memory which did not belong in so perfect a moment, and return to that which she truly desired.

Yet something about the phantasm her memory had managed to hold onto stayed her gaze. The brown and burning fierceness of those eyes; the warped ridge of a nose, marking like gravestones all the times its length had been broken; the scars swept in pale lines across his face, sharp as the strokes of so many quills dipped in searing ink. Without realizing it, Emrasarie felt her heart reaching towards it – towards *him* – and not for the lustful expressions splashed so shallowly upon those who reached out for her in the present.

"Uralant," she whispered.

A cold shock seized at her flesh. Suddenly realizing how little space still separated her from these nameless strangers, Emrasarie threw up her arms in protest before either could entreat her further. The rebuke succeeded in stalling both the man and woman, who stared at her with blank incomprehension, as if the notion of forgoing the desire bursting in their own hearts was all but foreign in their conceit of the world. When at last they gleaned naught of what they wanted would come from Emrasarie, she seemed to all but vanish from their awareness, and the two fell wordlessly into each other's arms instead.

Sweet and noxiously perfumed air spilled down her throat as she struggled to stand. She stumbled away from the pair's disport, arms and legs trembling as if stolen of all the strength they once possessed. The voice deeper than her thoughts, the pervasive drone babbling as if it belonged to this very place, urged her not to dwell on this interruption her beloved had caused, and to purge from her mind such unpleasant company and outwardly distractions. It followed behind her every step, insistent she remain stranded in the delirium induced by so abundant a stream of willing and rapacious delight as currently surrounded her.

Trying to swat away its influence as best she could, Emrasarie realized she had no memory of actually arriving here at all, her clarity of mind frayed as if to useless tatters. In their place bristled the echoes of rough and fibrous material pulled against her hands. A rope she had handled? Binding it with utmost haste to some out of sight area along the exterior deck? Where exactly that had been, or how she'd managed to avoid detection all the while, remained a disquieting blur. So too were the steps taken to then enter wherever upon the Ark this place existed, and the subsequent path which led her to the silken grass spread like a hundred pillows beneath her. A dim heat bristled in the muscles of her legs, as remains after one has danced heartily and with abandon, while the succulent flavors of a grand feast lingered on the tip of her tongue. Yet the recollection of having partaken in any of these endeavors eluded her, their absence spread like a gaping wound at the forefront of her awareness.

Against the cold such vacant and unremembered gulfs instilled, Emrasarie could but shiver, clutching desperately at her arms and the goosepimples riddled across them. She had to remind herself with every breath that this garden had not always been the entirety of her existence; that on the far side of those mist-occluded reaches, there waited a whole other world she was still a part of, and a person with whom she had shared so much of that same life with.

But so too did the sorcerer Zelaeus lurk there as well. His shadow tore like an infection through her then, and suddenly it was the dark sheen of his leering vizard breaching its way into her mind, the frigid artifice of so severely sculpted a face eviscerating all that was preciously human, preciously flawed, of her beloved. With every second it grew closer, creeping towards her with the same malevolence so many others had done so before it, their lips pursed in expectation, breath rank with desire, so eager to swallow her up whole.

She would have screamed in response had not the voice, that voice stemmed as if from the garden itself, done so first. It wailed and trumpeted and bemoaned in a fervor only she could hear, pleading for ignorance from all the fear she carried, all the pain which festered in her past, so that she might seek only for these pleasures of the here and now.

The shrieking weight proved too much for Emrasarie to bear. She had just reached a tall cypress set atop a hill when her strength abandoned her, and she collapsed beside a bed of roots breaking through the ground like long and grasping fingers.

Sprawled out on her back, she breathed in air made heavy by the warmth of increasingly potent incense. Above, the cypress boughs drooped in the stilled air. The leaves crowned atop them, sharp and angular as arrowheads, were engorged to such a degree that their verdancy gleamed a shade closer to black than green. Unable to free her gaze, she watched as their faces all but inhaled the light cast upon them, until it appeared to Emrasarie she was staring through scattered holes eaten across the very tapestry of creation itself, and into the Oblivion lurking on its farthest side. She could feel herself slipping into those abyssal depths; feel all her worry, her fear, the heartache which had so crippled her, whisked into so many shimmering pools absolute in their emptiness.

Uralant's face began to slip away with them too.

Laughter then broke upon her ears, mirth that was as an exuberant flood sweeping across woefully parched and sabulous earth. Footsteps followed close behind, and soon did Emrasarie find herself surrounded by a flock of revelers similar to those she had earlier left. They had paraded up the same hill as she, and now fell playfully to the grass about her, as if flower petals cast aside by an infatuate pondering the affection carried their way by the one whom they so ardently desired.

Emrasarie had not the strength, nor indeed the will, to retreat this time. She simply watched as arms fumbled lazily through the air, legs entwined with one another, and faces alight with the unearthly fire overhead coalesced like streams of wax dripping from a weary candle. The other face, so prevalent in her mind's eye only a moment ago, had completely disappeared. With it went the name it carried, and the affection she had felt towards it. Nothing remained in the void of its absence. Nothing but beauty seeking to smother her in its embrace. Beauty so much more preferable to all that was ugly, coarse, and unforgiving in the world beyond.

A shudder then passed through the bodies about her. Something from afar had drawn their attention away, so that it trickled like the first drops of rain before a storm down the hill they'd all climbed.

There, a rounded marble slab protruded from the earth, shining as an island of purest white amidst a sea of verdant swells. Other participants of the Frolic had similarly assembled so as to better observe this spot as well, and Emrasarie knew it must be a stage of some kind, upon which a performance was likely to begin. A sliver of black suddenly ripped through the diameter of the stage and began to widen, until a full aperture, leading to areas unseen and unlighted beneath the Ark, was opened.

So great was her anticipation, so fascinated was she by what might next follow, Emrasarie did not notice the subtle pinprick upon her arm, nor the sensation of something very small and very sharp sinking into the skin along her wrist. She could have never torn her eyes away to inspect the dull pain which lingered just above her hand as a shape was presently revealed there. Instead, she sought to devour with all her senses what had drifted up to take its place upon the stage.

A silhouette come to life, she thought; a figure tall and proud in stature, though wholly obscured behind a billowing cloak of purest sable. Only its head, smooth and luminous as a pearl freshly plucked from the prison of its shell, remained visible to the now deathly stilled audience. Emrasarie watched as the mouth then opened wide, wider, wider still, until at last there ushered forth from the shining and sensuous face a pitch beyond the pale trappings of mortal understanding, a preterhuman wail which struck at and caressed the very air through which it swelled.

She lost herself then. Her mind and body alike were swept away in a tidal wave of words so alien to the ears, so ponderous and decadent in what they hinted at, that it was as if the waking world itself was wholly shattered beneath their weight, and she could do naught but disappear into unfathomable realms of deepest sleep.

VII

THE journey to the Ark proved more arduous than Uralant would have initially guessed. Whether by some inscrutable aspect of the vessel's design, or the way its sharp edges seemed to shift and disappear within the mist still trailing off its sides, his perception of the distance still separating them from their intended target was somehow drastically warped, and he was rowing long after he expected they should have arrived.

Every arc his paddle cut became a grueling endeavor to overcome. Not only had he to contend with the weight of what felt like three passengers (the arachyne easily weighing the same as an adolescent upon his back) against a stubbornly stagnant current, there now pressed against him the tightening grip of self-doubt in light of the task set ahead, given shape by the grandeur of the Ark and its titanic walls that gobbled up more and more of the world from view. The structure, its façade even more daunting when viewed from so close a vantage, towered above as if a burnished curtain fallen down from infinity itself. As they continued their approach, it was only by keeping his eyes leveled directly ahead that Uralant did not plummet up those steel cataracts soaring to the sky and crash against the skewering peaks of vertigo waiting at their ends.

He grunted in defiance, redoubling his efforts even as muscles burned and spirit wavered.

By the time they reached the rope Emrasarie had left, exhaustion had withered away at Uralant's arms and stolen almost all the strength they carried. Zelaeus, meanwhile, suffered no such weariness. He impatiently scooped up the waiting rope when it came close enough to grab, and like a spider scurrying across its web did the sorcerer begin to climb. Breathing deep, Uralant summoned what few reserves of stamina were left to him and presently followed. Heave after straining heave drew him closer to the deck by maddeningly small degrees, until, with a final bestial grunt, he threw himself over the rim and fell on his side to the wonderfully firm footing of a solid floor.

"On your feet," the sorcerer hissed at Uralant, even as the curt exhalations of his own words betrayed the toll such an effort had similarly taken upon him. "We must be swift, lest wandering eyes catch us where we ought not to be."

Resisting the urge to respond, Uralant struggled to his feet with silent resolve. It took but a moment for much of his lost fortitude to return, and, freeing his blade from its scabbard, he shuffled along after Zelaeus.

An uneasy stillness filled the air as they stole with furtive steps across the vacant terrace on which the amphitheater rested. It reminded Uralant of the hush which patrols in solemn reverence the sealed doors of sepulchers forgotten to all but the lonely dead who inhabit them, and after several moments had passed without altercation, he realized they were the only passengers still outside the Vyrkylian structure. No hurrying trail of last-minute attendees. No patrolling guards. No sign of those cloaked rowers or their gondolas.

A cursory search made it clear the only entrance to the amphitheater was a tall and narrow tunnel facing the open deck from which the Ark's approved passengers had initially boarded. Uralant approached warily, unable to shake the impression that the way forward opened like a shrieking maw before them, as equally abstruse in its soaring and strangely faceted design as the walls through which it burrowed. No defensive force or restrictive barrier rose in opposition to them as they neared; only the dark innards waiting further ahead, their depths swirling with viscously opaque mist.

Zelaeus moved through without pause, the tread of his soles immediately dampened to soft murmurs as he all but vanished within. Glancing up at the arched entryway, its border adorned with icons of fearsome gryphons reared in majestic flight, Uralant wondered what had crossed his beloved's mind upon standing here, on the precipice of the unknown, oblivious as he was now towards what might be waiting at its end.

They had taken but a few dozen steps into the unlit passage when Uralant noticed the change. It was as if all sensation of the world had been stolen from awareness, leaving but a crushing emptiness to clamor about his ears. Lucrauna, the Ingroliths, indeed the very semblance of the world he'd always known, all suddenly seemed to him unimaginably distant, vague adumbrations at the end of a rapidly receding memory. Soon, what little light still reached them from without had been thoroughly bled of its brightness, and Uralant could see naught ahead save a faint glow. Repellently similar in shade to freshly spilled blood, it lacked any of the warmth cast by natural flame, and flared more intensely the closer they drew.

The outline of an open threshold took shape amidst the nothingness they had so far traversed, and Uralant steeled himself as they passed through, uncertain what to expect.

Whereas the passageway before had stretched in sensation as a near total void, the space into which they entered seethed with such an excess of sensory stimuli Uralant almost collapsed from their all-encompassing barrage. Several seconds passed before the panoply of sights, sounds, and smells came together and formed the impression of a garden in his mind, more picturesque than any painting, more perfect than any rhymed and lilting bucolic. Enclosed by walls that shot sheer towards a covered sky, and which were pockmarked along their bases by small grates leaking thin streams of a rapidly dissipating fog, the circular lawn sloped gently downward like the well of a shallow bowl, though one whose depths were cut with the ridges of small, cypress-topped hillsides. The dark reddish glow seen from the tunnel, Uralant now realized, came from a vast array of blazing shards strung up like garland strands across a series of arched rafters overhead, and which bathed the environs below in the otherworldly luster of their luminescence.

Yet it was not the sanguine effulgence which brought upon Uralant so unsettling a sense of disquiet. Nor was it the total absence of all the scattered noises which so normally compose nighttime's unending song. It was not even the bodies he now saw, those same beautiful bodies he had earlier glimpsed from afar, now lying prone across the grassy hills and in varying stages of undress, utterly lost to the waking world. It was something in the air itself. Something hostile and unknown. Something which should not have been allowed to exist upon this world, and which no living soul, who valued all that was passionate, capricious, and even fallible in their humanity, should have ever dared to seek after.

"Such sorcery at work here!" mused Zelaeus beside him, breaking the spell cast upon him and returning Uralant to the situation at hand. "Such power at its command!"

"At this moment?"

"All around us. What purpose it aims for, I cannot say; but so volatile a performance surely requires a master of the arts!"

Uralant gripped tighter his sword. "Does it bode ill for us?" he asked.

From the heavy folds of his cloak, the sorcerer drew a sword of his own. Next to Uralant's, the weapon was of a supremely narrow, almost delicate countenance, so thin it resembled more a reed plucked from some far away marshland than an instrument forged with the fury of war in mind. Wondering how something so meager could hope to contend in any type of combat, Uralant was thusly answered when a mumbled phrase from Zelaeus forced its lengthy edge to suddenly split apart and unfurl into a writhing tangle of viciously sharpened points. Through the air the long stalks gnashed and stung, swaying like an ornery viper horde unleashed from their den.

Uralant instinctively retreated several paces away, fearful their seemingly blind fervor might strike out against him.

"Were I not present, perhaps," the sorcerer cackled. "But I have been trained and instructed by the Queen Empyreal herself, who holds such power at her command as has not been possessed for a millennia. There is no equal to her in all this wide world, and therefore no equal to me."

Zelaeus then plunged headlong into the garden. Uralant, despite the warmth in the air he breathed, felt himself shiver. He forced himself to follow, desperate to find Emrasarie amidst these sleeping crowds, and fearful as to what might have transpired here before their arrival.

Over each hillock and rolling lawn they traversed, not one figure of the near hundredfold they saw was found cognizant. Whatever had brought them to such a state, it had affected all of them equally. Their faces, before bright and afire with excitement of what was to come, now shone dull and unresponsive, lost to an abeyance more arresting than anything Uralant had ever before witnessed. He did not see joy or happiness in any of those he passed, which he might have thought the ultimate goal in a Frolic such as this to be. Instead, their bodies were strewn limp and unresponsive, so that he might have believed himself looking at the mere husks of what had once been people, rather than the ineluctable slumber it so appeared.

His heart now thrashed against his chest like a captured manticore in its cage, fearful all the more of what condition he would thereby find Emrasarie in.

When at last they came to what seemed the nexus of the garden, there rose a wide, circular stage of marble, the first sign of construction they had so far seen. Zelaeus suddenly struck at the earth with his writhing sword, ripping up and sending a thin shower of soil through the air.

"This cannot be all there is," the sorcerer growled, his mask flashing as if in reflection to the anger laden in his voice. "There has to be somewhere it is kept. Somewhere on this infernal vessel not visible to us here."

Uralant had no answer. There had been no books in the Aphelaeum, no grueling bout in the fighting pits below Byrethlia, nor any fool-hardy emprise he and his beloved had embarked upon, which might have prepared him for this. There were forces at work here greater than the scope of what he might conceive, and the longer they remained within such a domain, the more Uralant feared they might not ever escape.

It was then, eyes alert for any threat as they stood exposed in the open, that Uralant caught the telltale shimmer of golden tresses from atop a nearby hill, bright even beneath the incarnadine glow which so suffused the air. Ignoring all else, he bolted up the slope, legs straining against the weight of the arachyne. The cerulean shade well familiar to him was soon clear amidst a carpet of other half-worn raiment, as well as the heartbreakingly beautiful face awaiting at its top.

"Emrasarie!" Uralant gasped, only just preventing himself from shouting out her name. He leapt around the equally oblivious persons who shared the shade beneath the hilltop tree, and dropped beside her sleeping form.

Even after witnessing so many others lost in similarly unconscious states, it still shocked Uralant to behold just how far away his beloved seemed in her slumber, how distant she felt simply lying there unresponsive. Fearful of waking her lest he cause some sort of lasting damage which could not then be mended, or that she might remain unresponsive despite all his efforts, Uralant felt his hands shaking even as he brushed aside stray locks of hair from her face and pulled back up the shoulder of her dress from where it had tumbled down. He then noticed a faint shimmer trailing away from her wrists.

There were cords of a supremely thin, almost wire-like make, firm though malleable in composition, sunken into the softness of her skin. From some unseen source in the grass beyond they snaked up to her, and taking them gingerly in hand, Uralant found they were not unlike the spools of necromantic twine he had previously used to rouse unearthed corpses into cadaverons. Yet whereas that material was wrapped around its subjects so as to bring forth a potent, albeit spurious imitation of life, these sank like vampyric fangs into the flesh of their victims, and had drained away all animating spirit until only this death-like stillness remained.

Balking at such gruesome instrumentation, Uralant tore away each of the loathsome strands from Emrasarie. He winced as they slid free from her like needles being passed through cloth, leaving but the smallest pinpricks of blood behind, before he cast them to the ground in disgust. When at last she lay free of their marring touch, Uralant gently lifted Emrasarie until she was cradled in his arms, her body limp and fragile as a porcelain doll.

A sharp stab of panic pressed upon his heart when she did not immediately stir. Then, just as he grew desperate enough to consider the sorcerer's aid, a sudden gasp of air rushed through Emrasarie's lips. The crushing torpor under which she had previously been buried was shed from her shoulders, and she jerked upright within his arms, her eyes wide as if waking from the grasp of an unspeakable nightmare.

"Uralant!" she exclaimed when the shock subsided and she recognized him. Throwing her arms around his shoulders, she squeezed as if he were the sole piece of flotsam still afloat in the aftermath of a shipwreck, the only thing that might prevent her from drowning in the tumultuous waters she'd found herself stranded. "I...couldn't remember. I couldn't remember *you*. One moment you were there in my thoughts, and the next you vanished, as if I'd somehow forgotten you. How? How could I do such a thing?"

"Great sorcery is at work here, my love," he said softly. "And dark designs we do not yet understand."

"We?" Emrasarie stiffened. "He is here with you?"

The sound of footsteps fast approaching answered before Uralant could. The sorcerer's robes swept to a halt behind them, and he waited there, glowering with the stance of an executioner waiting to deliver at last the killing blow.

"As touching a reunion as this seems, need I remind you both of the severity of your debt? We have yet to find what I seek, and should you wish your lives spared, I suggest you not tarry here for long."

"She needs but a moment's rest before we proceed," Uralant growled. With a gentleness which belied the severity of his tone, he assisted her to her feet, noting how her legs yet wobbled uncertainly beneath.

The sorcerer chortled. "Perhaps you have forgotten, dear *friends*, the dangers you face on this night are twofold: one which remains unknown, but another whose threats have been demonstrated with utmost clarity time and time again."

Uralant remained unwavering as stone. He stood his ground between the sorcerer and his beloved even as the stalks of that writhing blade cut through the very air before him, and the arachyne's claws seemed to pierce with bristling sharpness at his chest.

"Please, stop this!" pleaded Emrasrie. "I am well, my love! You need not worry yourself over me. Already I feel much improved, and wish to continue on."

"And how fortunate for us," Zelaeus snapped.

Before any search could be resumed, however, the sorcerer suddenly went rigid in stance before them. The dark pits in his mask were beholden to something on the ground, something near the spot where Emrasarie had lain. Following his gaze, Uralant saw naught at first; then he too noticed the rustling within the long grass, like snakes slithering in speedy pursuit after some unseen prey afar, and witnessed the freed cords he had pulled from his beloved's wrists, previously motionless, now being drawn away from where they'd been abandoned.

The sorcerer scrambled after the receding wires. Uralant followed. They came to the tree trunk under whose branches Emrasarie had slept, the other revelers still piled about in benumbed heaps at their feet, and just managed to catch the cord's tail ends as they slipped away through little recesses in the gnarled tangle of roots, so small as to nearly be imperceptible on first glance. Closer inspection revealed many similar gaps grown across the cypress base, out of which came a whole series of the strand-like material.

It took but a few seconds to confirm what they already suspected: each of the visible wires were, in turn, attached to the slumbering figures nearby, and suckled like a swarm of leeches at flesh lying utterly exposed for their pleasure. A feast wholly acquiescent of its fate.

A thousand and more questions bellowed in Uralant's mind to be answered, yet when he opened his mouth to give them form, the words previously clamoring to be released failed him. "What is the meaning of this?" was all he managed to utter.

Cold silence, trailing like a specter their abject and total confusion, was his only answer for a span. Then, Zelaeus spun around and cast the gleaming ire set upon his mask towards Emrasarie.

"You were present here; you partook in the Frolic," he said, voice so terse as to be accusatory. "Perhaps you are now in possession of such an answer, and would fain reveal those truths to us."

It took but a glance her way for Uralant to know she remained in the same shadows of ignorance he and the sorcerer resided as well. She looked at him with a haunted expression, her pallor turned a nauseous hue at the thought of having been afflicted the same as these oblivious souls. When she thusly attempted to relay what had transpired, her voice quavered at every half-started and ultimately abandoned memory, their contents little more than a confused collection of intense, yet frustratingly vague sensations unable to shed further understanding on the events at hand.

One detail, however, did stand out, though whether due to its surprising clarity compared to what preceded it, or because of what it might portend were it true, Uralant could not say. Regardless, he listened intently as Emrasarie recounted the sparse impressions of a performance that had occurred upon the distant stage; a singular, all-together arresting act put on by a personage unlike any she had ever seen. One who, by the sheer prominence imparted and influence exuded, must surely be the one wielding the strings behind this Frolic, this Ark, perhaps all of Lucrauna itself.

"They were...strange. So very strange. I could see them there on the stage, clear as I see you now. Yet I cannot recall whether they were man or woman in nature, youthful or elderly in age. All I can remember is that they were...beautiful," she paused, and her brow furrowed as if in sudden confusion. "Beautiful...I think? Or maybe terrifying? Oh, I cannot say. They were both, somehow, wearing a face that was not a face, and yet was all faces brought together into one."

"They are strong indeed, whoever this Numynaris is," Zelaeus muttered in response as he crouched to further inspect the cords below. "I have not heard of such a thing afore, nor witnessed any manner of sorcery like this from my Queen. Ah, what a prize it will be, when I claim and return to her the passages from which these feats were born!"

Uralant, meanwhile, grit his teeth in consternation, scouring nervously the garden that lay frozen as if the scene of a mural before his eyes. This place had been disconcerting since the moment they'd dared to board it, and only grew more intolerable the longer they remained within its unnatural confines.

How merciful would it be, he thought, for one of the many cypress boughs above to suddenly snap free from its perch and plummet atop the sorcerer, crushing him beneath its weight before any foul tricks could be used in response! Freed from his malign influence, the two of them would have no reason to linger on in so horrid a place, and could retreat the way they'd come without fear of reprisal lurking in their wake. They might then resign this night to the unpleasant memory it had been, a dream to be readily forgotten.

"Oh, how devious!" the sorcerer's cackle rang so sharp Uralant flinched. "So intent were we upon the wires flowing forth, we did not observe in full the tree from which they stemmed!"

Rising to his feet, Zelaeus lowered his weapon and placed his free palm upon the tree in question's surface. More foul words were uttered, words which repulsed Uralant the more he continued to hear them, and there then appeared a dark stain at the spot he touched. Resembling in shade the severe hue of a grievous bruise, the discoloration crept across the tree face like a withering disease, until it reached a full two meters in height. Then, as if by a final command from Zelaeus, the blighted area suddenly drained out of existence itself, leaving but a crude and caustic hole where once had been solid matter. A hole which led into a hollowed, artificially constructed space within.

"We stand here upon a lie," he proclaimed. "And being so thorough a fabrication, what then is it attempting to conceal?"

Rooted in place by the feat just performed, and by what its implication hinted at towards the very ground beneath them, Uralant and Emrasarie watched as the sorcerer stuck his head within the newly created aperture. When he turned back, it was as if the silver smile of his mask beamed with newfound enmity towards them, and Uralant shivered when Zelaeus then raised a finger towards him.

"Come; you first."

VIII

THE arachyne's claws tightened when Uralant did not immediately obey. Unwilling to further tempt its wrath, he forced himself forward and into the gaping portal ahead. As he bent low and squeezed into the opened space within, he felt not only its awkward weight against him, but also the weight of the sorcerer's own myopic desire right at his neck, its insistence continuing to send them deeper and ever more unprepared into perilous realms of the unknown.

A sort of scaffolding met Uralant's outstretched hand. Its interconnecting bars formed the rudimentary struts of a ladder, which led far below and out of sight. Hearing the sharp groan of steel struggling to bear his weight, Uralant began to tentatively descend, bracing himself for whatever might lurk in the shadows beneath their feet.

Presently did the unnatural light overhead fade from view, so that Uralant found himself nearly blinded by the blackness into which he was submerged. Yet as the last bits of scaffolding disappeared beneath him, replaced by a hard floor on which he could stand, he realized that for as heavy as the obfuscating shroud fallen across him initially appeared, it was not, in fact, absolute.

On all sides there shimmered and blinked little pinpricks of illumination throughout the miasmal veil. They cast into that abyss colors of a kind he did not recognize, and which seemed to him, just as those in the garden sky above, void of the intrinsic warmth begot by burning flame. These, instead, glistened akin to gemstones set atop a gilded crown, and though they coruscated only dimly, their numbers were so profuse Uralant's vision slowly acclimated, bringing shape to the otherwise shapeless gloom.

Such was the chamber's size into which he'd entered, and the great lengths to which it spanned, that Uralant wondered whether the Ark they had invaded was in truth some manner of beast beyond the sale of mortal men to comprehend, and if he had just been swallowed into the very bowels of its stomach. Like a great ossein latticework did the columns, joists, and rafters rise up around him, their surfaces gleaming with the cold sinews of woven and burnished steel. Obelisks and strangely-shaped pedestals were scattered about in every direction, and he saw it was on these so many of the coldly twinkling lights were inlaid. Some remained inert and silent as stone, while others emitted soft droning sounds, along with occasional gusts of frigid winds from their sides. When one of these exhalations struck Uralant square upon the face, he reeled from the acrid stench which assailed his nostrils, sharp as the points of ruthlessly polished steel daggers.

Stumbling backwards, he nearly fell when something on the floor got tangled about his feet. It was a mass of those same wires from above, having spilled down the scaffolded shaft he'd climbed, and which now trailed openly across the floor.

Whereas before he had only seen the strands as single rivulets or cascading little streams, Uralant now beheld a flood spread beneath him. Collected from similar shoots and access points no doubt hidden all across the garden above, the agglutination of so many disparate tendrils beneath him resembled the vision caught of veins when flesh is peeled back from muscle, and the nakedness underneath is revealed. The weaving currents they formed came together at what appeared to be the chamber's center, corresponding exactly, he thought, to where the stage had been set overhead, and fed into a series of tall, oddly transparent columns which circled around the nexus like monoliths erected around a temple's most sacred ground.

Warily approaching the nearest one, Uralant suddenly drew back, his shocked intake of breath cutting like a sharp and thunderous clap through the pervasive silence.

They were filled with blood. Vibrantly fresh and ever-increasing quantities of blood.

What little warmth his body still retained vanished. Retreating to the scaffolding he had come down, Uralant could feel his heart slamming against his chest, hear the blood surging through his head as it searched in vain for some respite from the cold slivers of fear that assailed it. What use could be gained from so abhorrent a machination, he dared not guess. Nor could he imagine the manner of devil this Numynaris must be to desire so repulsive a prize.

He had just reached the lowest of the connected bars when a creaking sound echoed through the broad, shadow-drenched chamber. Fearing an ambush, Uralant raised his sword, muscles instinctually falling into a fighting stance. Yet he could see no shapes moving amidst the darkness. When the noise continued, louder than before, he glanced aloft, and there saw Emrasarie scaling down the same way he'd come, Zelaeus and his rippling alb of black close behind.

"Stay close to me," he whispered when her feet at last touched to the floor, and she too bore witness to all that lurked here beneath the garden's lush, ultimately shallow veneer.

"What is this place?" her voice sounded too small in the sprawling enormity, too liable to become lost in the shadows which pressed so hungrily on all sides of them.

"I know not," spoke Uralant truthfully as he guided her clear from where the sorcerer was fast approaching from above, and away from the blood-brimming columns he'd been unfortunate enough to glimpse. "But whatever it is, we must find a way to be free of it, the sorcerer be damned. We have passed beyond the scope of what we might hope to contend with. These are realms darker and more sinister than any we have tread before, and I will not see either of us brought to harm by the whims of a madman."

"But what of the thing still bound to you? Will he not awaken its wrath should you make any move against him?"

"I will find a moment to strike when he has no such chance."

"You cannot take that risk!" she hissed, gripping at his arm. "I will not see you harmed on account of so reckless a gamble!"

They were forced to silence then, as the resounding thud of Zelaeus landing upon the floor nearby echoed with the heavy timber of fortress gates slammed shut.

"We have no choice, should either of us hope to survive." So quiet was Uralant's voice, even he struggled to find comfort in its utterance.

The sorcerer, meanwhile, was succumb to an awed silence as he beheld their new surroundings. He moved slowly between the block-shaped structures blinking and shimmering without any apparent function, and made his way towards the array of columns rising up like crimson idols waiting to be worshipped. Looking upon the blood they so gluttonously coveted, he came to a halt, captivated not with fear or disgust, Uralant thought, but something closer to reverential wonder as he stared upon them.

Stared with his back fully exposed and open to attack.

Uralant squeezed the hilt of his sword and, with as delicate a step as he could muster, stalked behind his path. Amidst so stark an absence of light, the mask Zelaeus wore had, for the first time, been drained to a dull and lackluster countenance, little more than a crowned façade of gray. Its once gleaming angles were now flattened, so thoroughly as to appear a mockery of their previous grandeur, and had been robbed the aura of invincibility its presence had heretofore conveyed. If ever had the moment to strike down and fell an enemy had been presented to Uralant, this was it. He was so close now; almost within his blade's long reach.

"Uralant!"

The cry from Emrasarie tore all thought of the sorcerer and his impending demise clear from thought. Spinning round, Uralant saw his beloved's face gone aghast, her arm extended out and pointing to something in the darkness beyond.

Through the shadows did a figure slide towards where he and Zelaeus stood. Like a demoniac skeleton it appeared, tall and gaunt of shape, its body possessed of a dark sheen and sharply angled edges which glinted menacingly in the sparse light. A narrow, perfectly elliptical head sat upon craned neck and rigid shoulders, and when it jerked around to better view them, Uralant saw not a pair of eyes glaring out from its featureless face, but instead a single large orb of preternaturally burning red.

With frightening haste did this demon then throw itself towards him. The stiff and severe way in which it scurried ahead reminded Uralant of the gondola rowers along the Amaranthyn from earlier, their movements similarly abrupt and unnatural, and he lamented for his own sake their shedding of those mercifully concealing cloaks. Against such a foe, the weight of his sword remained reassuring when all else familiar had been thrown to the wayside, the one thing ever under his control and to be relied upon.

The demon suddenly launched into the air, taloned hands outstretched like ballistae missiles aimed straight at his heart. Roaring in response, Uralant made ready to meet it with the full strength of a slashing blow. His muscles afire with anticipation, there then flashed across his vision long streaks of stabbing gray, and his enemy was brought to an impromptu stop. Not thrown back or dropped down to the floor, but simply stopped, its body dangling uselessly right where it had been in the arc of its flight, skewered through by the fingers of the sorcerer's many-headed blade.

"My, my; from what segment of the Scrawl were you dreamt out of, I wonder?" exclaimed Zelaeus as he strode into view. With a twist of his wrist the piercing needles retracted, and were brought back to their previously coiling and amorphous shapes. Released from its impalement and gone rigidly limp, the creature's body crashed with a metallic thud to the floor and did not move again. "Oh-ho, and you have friends who wish to play as well!"

Sure enough, more of the demons had appeared, identical in every aspect to the first, and were shambling forth from whatever shadowy cage had once kept them contained. Though the main bulk of the number directed their attack towards the sorcerer, Uralant spied several that had veered aside and were instead making towards Emrasarie. Leaping with furious bounds, he hurled himself across the distance separating them, and thrust like a battering ram his sword at the nearest threat. Its length plunged clear through the enemy's torso, releasing a heavy spume of embers from its back as it crumpled from the blow and collapsed.

Quickly pulling his weapon free, Uralant noted a thick, glistening fluid of purest black now coated its tapered edges, bearing a gaseous stench that lingered even as he leapt clear from a subsequent attack. More talons cut through the air in a whirlwind of steel, and as Uralant dodged about and kept the slashing monstrosity at bay, he realized no other sounds came from any of these approaching demons. No roars or shrieks of fury, no grunted breaths from exertion, no muttered curses or vows of vengeance for its fallen companion; just the tearing of its hands through empty space, and red eyes glaring at him, bright as the blood they were so desperate to spill.

Spying an opening, Uralant took the chance and swung high. He felt the shattering of steel beneath steel, and the subsequent tear as a rigid neck was severed through. When the head finally fell and crashed near his feet, the eye set within it dimmed to a vacant black, and did not ignite again.

Zelaeus, meanwhile, seemed in near ecstatic spirits as more still flooded against him, cackling and twirling about as he hacked and cut at the demons with ruthless, unrelenting glee. "Is this it? Is this all the challenge you offer? Such useful pawns you might be, had you a proper master behind your construction! Come now, I see the scrying eyes aflame within your skulls; I know the secrets behind such ancient and entheal arts! Let us see who lurks behind this sorcery! Let us witness Numynaris!"

Uralant cursed. Before any more of the demons could reach them, he grabbed hold of Emrasarie's hand and pulled them away. Without a weapon, his beloved was all but defenseless there in the open, and it would be folly attempting to defend both himself and her from so many an oncoming threat. Weaving round pedestals and other misshapen obtrusions, he led them towards the grove of columns that had so repelled him earlier. Though he still dreaded to look upon and ponder what their purpose might be, the tightly packed and clustered pattern their formation made might offer some manner of protection against the fiendish mob in pursuit.

They reached the outermost of the cylindrical monuments with not a moment to spare. Emrasarie slipped through a gap between two of their towering forms just as the scurried clatter of metallic feet swelled behind them. Uralant held his ground, swinging about with the full weight of his sword in tow.

The blade cleaved a devastating arc as it flew wide and fast, so fast the closest demon could not avoid its cutting edge, and found its chest battered down into a mangled ruin. A second swiveled clear of the strike, while a third leapt overtop the newly fallen carcass. With seemingly no thought for strategy or tactics, they swarmed upon him simultaneously, seeking to overwhelm him rather than best him in any manner of combat.

He gave them no such chance. Sidestepping to the left, he cleared their attack by a hair's breadth, before striking back at the nearest figure. He then kicked the staggered demon straight into its realigning companion, toppling them both and allowing him the chance to deliver killing thrusts down to each in quick succession.

Spitting at their broken carcasses, Uralant abandoned the wider chamber and delved after Emrasarie into the narrow path cut between so many blood-filled columns. Their number stretched further than he had initially guessed, growing like a forest full of broad vermillion trunks rather than just a simple grove, and there reared within him the faintest whisper of fear he had somehow become lost within their labyrinthine depths.

When at last he burst free from the infernal grip of their presence, any relief he might have felt was quickly dashed by the sight of Emrasarie, still beneath the shadows cast by those towering pillars, now petrified in place, as if she were terrified to fully enter the fuliginous glade waiting ahead.

He followed her wide-eyed gaze. Darkness more tangible than any shadow should be was draped before them, stealing all which might have lurked beneath it from view, save for the table not ten paces away. Bulky in design, it emitted a wan light from its level face, warding back the tenebrous shroud festering so thoroughly from all sides.

Uralant took a step towards the table. There, beneath a flawless sheet of glass, he glimpsed three pieces of parchment, all torn, singed, and crumbling in decay, set beneath the glass, each riddled with the black-inked scrawlings of a language he had not the slightest familiarity with. When he made to venture closer still, Emrasarie's hand suddenly closed tight around his wrist.

"We should not be here," her voice trembled as she spoke. An ashen mask had fallen upon her face, a terror fixated on something lurking further within the shadows, something Uralant had not initially seen. "We are not alone."

Peering deeper, Uralant caught the faintest hint of a silhouette there, a massive shape seated atop what by closest comparison alone might have been called a throne, when a vice-like grip suddenly squeezed against his chest. The pressure from the arachyne's claws attacked with such ferocity that he felt as if a sundered tree had crashed atop him, threatening to break his spine and steal from his lungs the very air they so desperately needed. Gasping for breath and nearly overwhelmed by the pain, he felt more than saw the impact as he dropped helplessly to his knees.

"Back...away...now," a voice made breathless by the fervor of slaughter ordered, and Uralant saw through squinted eyes Emrasarie backing away as the sorcerer's foul outline came into view.

"You don't understand," she pleaded, hands raised in deference as Zelaeus trudged past her with writhing sword still in hand and made for the table nearby. "Our aim was not-"

"To what? Betray me?" Zelaeus whirled about to face them. The dark pits of his mask burned all the more terribly next to the stains of greasy black liquid now splattered across it. His albs were rent and cut to tatters in places, but he appeared otherwise unharmed. Indeed, he bellowed a cruel shriek of laughter, before turning back to the table and placing a hand lovingly upon the glass there. "Oh, I know the thought must have crossed your minds, and many a time as well. But I am afraid the act of betrayal will be mine to undertake this evening. After all, your parts in this play have run the course of their usefulness. Anything further would but reduce you to a liability, and I will not suffer such obstacles when I have *these* precious gifts to bring back to my Queen! It has been so long since additional segments of the Vyryn Scrawl were reclaimed! So long since new sorcery flowed forth from her lips, and granted in turn to her faithful-"

Zelaeus fell silent then. The force which had been attempting to break through Uralant's chest vanished as the sorcerer's attention wandered from those scraps of parchment displayed there upon the table, and instead towards what lay within the darkness beyond.

Casting aside the heavy shadows draped across its silhouette, the monstrous shape seated there remained motionless no longer; slowly, and with sublime amenity, it had begun to stir.

IX

EMRASARIE realized then what was to come. Before the shadows had fully been shed from so titanic a stature, she knew what would presently emerge to greet them there. She remembered it having done so earlier upon the stage above, rising with all the vainglorious elan of a performer ready to entice an audience into believing with heart and mind alike the fabrication soon to follow. She shivered to think of how helplessly she had tumbled into the depths of that deceit, drowning as if a fly in the sweet nectar of overly ripened fruit. How glorious such a prospect had seemed then! How content she would have been to simply stifle there, allowing so delirious a fantasy to wash over her again and again, had not Uralant pulled her free from its hold!

She could not bear to face such an entity again.

"Hurry!" she pleaded her beloved. "We must make away from this place!"

Straining to his feet, Uralant nodded. Neither spared a single glance behind as there slid with malicious pomp the sound of footsteps ever closer towards them. Instead, the two plunged back the way they'd initially entered, Emrasarie's legs screaming as she ran, urging her to move faster and faster between the monuments to so many collected liters of blood, desperate to be as far from this accursed place as possible.

That cacophony, however, was not loud enough to smother the boasts she then heard as Zelaeus's bravado returned, directed now at the awakened specter of her dreams – her nightmares. The wild threats and taunts he threw were presently followed by a span of shocked quiescence from the sorcerer, there having echoed through the room the shrill clatter of his sword bouncing harmlessly against a metal too resilient to be cut, pierced, or broken.

Flooding into the emptiness of sound came a scream; a font of unleashed agony as she could have never before conceived possible. So deeply did its reverberations gouge into her ears that she might have collapsed in shock had not the self-preserving instinct for escape overwhelmed everything else. Tearing at her ears, it crescendoed to higher and more intolerable pitches of suffering, until at last it erupted with a muculent climax of what could only be flesh, sinew, and bone being pulled apart at their very seams. A subsequent splatter of viscera falling in scattered heaps across the floor left only silence in its wake, and Emrasarie found herself, despite all he had put them through, nearly offering unto the sorcerer the smallest sliver of pity for so gruesome a fate.

Any lingering notes of carnage had quieted by the time they slipped free from the last of the sanguine-faced pillars and into the broad exterior chamber. Instead, there now came an ominous tolling to their backs as enraged and armored footsteps surged in pursuit, closing fast the distance between.

She therefore quailed to see the dozen or so meters still separating them from the scaffold tower down which they had initially come. They would never reach it, nor be able to scale its height up towards the garden's dim light above, without leaving themselves fully exposed to the oncoming threat.

With precious seconds remaining, the two resorted to huddling behind one of the taller pedestals nearby, a hiding spot that could only temporarily forestall an inevitable conclusion. Grabbing hold of Uralant's hand, Emrasarie could but listen as footsteps like thunder ravaging the sky swelled perilously close to their position, the steel plates underfoot quivering as if in reciprocal fear.

Without warning, their pursuer then stopped. A lengthy silence fell upon the chamber, so pervasive Emrasarie worried her own haggard breath might give them away. She imagined cold, glassy eyes scouring with unwavering patience the surrounding shadows for where they might have fled. She could feel the simmering rage at the source of that gaze, feel the heaviness of so much hatred waiting to burst through the tenuous calm.

Then: "Another rat yet lingers in my home."

The voice assailed Emrasarie as if the lilting rhythm of waves swept along the shoreline; gentle on the surface, yet hinting at so much power underneath. Against her ears she threw the palms of both hands, squeezing shut at the same time her eyes in an attempt to better ward away the influence its intonations cast.

"I still smell its filth defiling my sanctuary."

The undeterred pacing of a search resumed cut through the air like the knelling of a ponderous bell.

"Where has it scurried off with you, my precious pet?"

It took greater resiliency than Emrasarie had counted on in suppressing the near insatiable urge to answer so intoxicating a call. The taste of copper drenched the inside of her mouth, and she realized her tongue was bleeding, pierced by teeth that had blindly bitten down in a valiant effort to resist.

Beside her, Uralant's face was contorted by a singularly confused expression. Unable to settle on either rapaciousness or disgust, he too bore witness to the sensory onslaught induced by so eloquent and unrelenting a speaker, and Emrasarie could see the sweat beading along his brow, the tightness hardening his jaw.

Yet for all those signs of uncertainty, there bristled bright in his eyes ever-defiant flames of rage, a fervor that would never be quieted so easily. Even in this most dire of circumstances, Uralant was still searching for an opportunity to attack.

"Our time together was not yet finished."

Emrasarie knew then what she must do. She took a deep breath, hoping some of the fear that had welled so high within her might spill over and clear her spinning head. Whether it worked or not, she could not say. Regardless, she reached out to her beloved and took his face in trembling hands so as to draw him close to her. Uralant's surprise lasted for but an instant, evaporating when she leaned further still and met him with a kiss. She allowed herself to savor that moment of intimacy in spite the danger lurking just out of sight, holding to her heart the flutter she felt even then, the binding truth of the love they shared.

"After all, you are still mine."

When at last she pulled away, the wretchedness of her mask was returned, and had forced onto her face a smile as sharpened at the edges as a scythe raised in preparation for its reaping strike. Turning from Uralant, she then crawled to the opposite end of the pedestal as him and stood up, revealing herself in full.

"I am here, Numynaris!" she said.

"Ah, so you are, my pet. And how truly beautiful you remain."

There, set so high atop a mantle of sheer obsidian her neck craned to meet its gaze, loomed the wielder of a physiognomy so close to perfect it almost proved painful to endure. Earlier amidst the Frolic, that face had spanned a distance from her as of pale Ilophrin waxing atop the firmament's highest vaults, a beneficent vision more spectral in beauty than fully lucid. Now, brought into such clarity she could see herself reflected in the waxen pools of those wide, staring eyes, Emrasarie beheld a torturer, one whose tools were lashes unfurling like black heron wings above those glistening oceans of sight; lips liable to swallow up the world in the flushed depths of their fullness; cheeks

97

like the summits of majestic, snow-capped mountains hinting at unknown paradises beyond. The coalescing of their totality together resulted in what was less a face and more a tessellated expression brought into being by a thousand distinct facets of disparate beauty, each warring so desperately against one another for dominance that the whole could not bear such an orgy of dimorphic qualities, and so had been smoothed into that of a flawless and uncannily-alluring epicene.

Just as she'd planned, the towering presence of Numynaris glided further towards her and away from the pedestal end where Uralant crouched. What she had not been prepared for was the unblinking intensity blazing within the depths of those eyes, nor the supple vibrancy of so vast and smothering a smile, seeking to forever entreat her back into the grip of its hypnotizing thrall. How easy it might be, she thought in spite herself, to again fall blindly into all the wanton delight promised in the perfect contours of that simulacrum! And how readily she might have cast herself back into the lustful depths of that dream, had not the truth of Uralant's touch still lingered upon her lips!

"Come to me now, so I may protect you from the verminous cur who has dared breach this, my sacred domain."

The command slithered through lips curling aberrantly behind the words they uttered. Emrasarie's legs froze, unable to either flee from or fall into the approaching embrace. She could but gape in teary-eyed silence as Numynaris drew nearer still, hoping beyond hope Uralant understood the chance given to him here.

As if in answer to her plea, there suddenly came a flash of movement from behind. Like an enraged bear did Uralant emerge, bounding ahead with sword raised high and letting loose a cry that was as an avalanche unleashed upon a mountainside. His weapon flew uncontested to strike at Numynaris's chest, a swing with such force behind its arcing path that Emrasarie knew it would sheer straight through the waist of an unarmored man, or mangle into useless ruin even the hard plate of cuirass steel.

Instead, the blow bounced to a halt when it struck, as if a wall of stone had risen to take his target's place.

Whether the heavy shadows which then fell across Uralant came from shock, or from Numynaris, who had swiveled around with lissome grace to glower at this most recent interruption, Emrasarie could not guess. She was aware only of her own heart as it skipped no less than several beats in response to this unforeseen impossibility.

"My, my," the epicene chuckled blithely at the long fray now rent across the midnight garb. "Such a paltry showing in the end."

Numynaris then threw back the sprawling mantle with so great a flourish its fabric swept through the air like monstrous wings in flight, battering Emrasarie with a sudden gust so strong she was nearly knocked to the floor. Revealed underneath was a slender body adorned entirely in gleaming plate, and the dark, livid luster of its impeccable craftsmanship marked it as the most precious and impervious of metals: orichalcum. Uralant's weapon, and likewise any weapon forged by common steel, could never have hoped to pierce through so rare and invulnerable a surface.

Lashing out with unobstructed arms, Numynaris swiped away Uralant's sword with the same indifference one might otherwise show a wooden stick, and slammed a mace-like gauntlet directly into his unguarded chest.

She shrieked as her beloved's body tumbled across the floor and came to a stop several meters away. Throwing herself past Numynaris, she dropped beside Uralant as he wheezed and struggled to his knees. Somehow, he remained unbroken even after so savage a strike. The arachyne, Emrasarie shuddered as her fingers brushed against the encasing metal arms, had inadvertently saved his life.

"Curious," the epicene mused.

When Emrasarie looked back, she saw their enemy hampered not by cumbrous armor and the restrictive confluence of so many intersecting segments, but approaching as if in the throes of an intricately rehearsed dance, plate sliding seamlessly over plate like rivulets of water rolling down a window pane. In the blink of an eye the epicene was upon them again, and Emrasarie shrieked in protest as Uralant was grabbed by the neck and hoisted into the air, so high his feet swung futilely above the ground below.

"What bothersome toys it brings along," said Numynaris, eyeing the arachyne bound to him with apathetic contempt.

Emrasarie couldn't move. It was if she were seared in place, even as Uralant dangled helplessly above her, totally and completely out of reach. Taking one of the arachyne's hooked arms in hand, his captor proceeded to pry at the appendage so severely that, bit by bit, it lost hold of Uralant's chest, bending outwardly and at a horrifyingly warped angle. Then, by a final wrenching tear, the claw broke with an ear-splitting snap from the cuneate base to which it had previously been attached.

Ignoring both her cries for mercy and Uralant's cries of agony, the epicene continued, boasting an increasingly exultant expression while the same process was repeated with each of the remaining arms.

"Cretinous fool. Can you even grasp how far I have risen beyond your lowly rank? I have, since afore you were a whisper in your ancestor's dreams, been shed the frail flesh of birth striking mankind moribund, able only to wither and, in the end, succumb to ash. For more lifetimes than can be counted have my vitals, housed now within this vastly superior form, gained succor from the inexhaustible fonts of blood that flock willingly to this Frolic, and the quickening arcana latent within their depths. Across a millennium's span have I labored in the creation of this last vestige of Vyrkylos, striving to taste even the smallest mote of splendor as my progenitors possessed, afore the Phlegethon hurled them from their empyrean seat of power and stole from me the inheritance of pleasures unimaginable in this decrepit, woeful age."

When the final arm was severed, Numynaris discarded Uralant to the floor, proclaiming: "And now, risen to such heights, a filth-riddled pest dares sully all I have wrought, and attempts to stain this, the only paradise left upon the world? Truly, does so gormless a rat hope to overcome and fell the mighty gryphon?"

Never before had Emrasarie seen her beloved brought so close to utter ruin. He lay there as if an insect whose wings and writhing legs had been plucked away by a cruel child giddy for a chance at tormenting something so much smaller, so infinitely weaker in every way, than themselves, and when the sharpened sole of Numynaris's solleret bore down upon Uralant's now naked back, it did so not with the impetus to immediately crush him, but to prolong his suffering to the point where he might beg for the embrace of Death rather than endure another minute of such misery.

"Stop!" she cried, ignoring the warm tears coursing down her cheeks, and the warmer blood drenching red her palms. The flesh there had been flayed by the armor she tried to pull back, its every inch brisling with filigree so intricately carved as to resemble the plumage of viciously barbed feathers. "Please, have mercy!"

Nothing. Her pleas vanished alongside Uralant's continued wailing, and Emrasarie, beating uselessly against the orichalcum pillars that continued their assault, feared all was lost. She had no means to overcome this seemingly invincible behemoth, no strength from which to draw nor plan to call upon. No way to pierce through what could not be broken. If Uralant's mighty sword, and all the force by which he'd wielded it, had been unable to even falter so insurmountable a foe, what hope did she possibly have?

Then, like lightning striking at the earth, there blazed within her a fiery wave of insight.

"Numynaris," she called gently, reaching out with bloodied hand and taking the clenched, gauntleted fist of her enemy in her grasp.

A noticeable shudder swept through the armored titan. "But a moment my pet. I will see to you once this wastrel is broken and its remains sent to slumber in the Amaranthyn below."

"Please, can Death not wait to claim him? Would you deprive me of the comfort I so desire, in light of the horror he has put me through?"

Eyes narrowing, Numynaris turned to look down at her, and Emrasarie could feel suspicion pointed like daggers from their depths. But there glimmered something else there as well; something frail, hopeful, and unmistakably human. "Speak, fairest of my flock. Who is this man to you? Has he not come to wrest you free from our Frolic?"

She took a deep breath, steadying herself so her mask would not shatter. Then: "But to steal me back! For years has this brute lusted after what he could not possess, following like a shadow my footsteps in hopes of one day winning a favor I never sought to give. Desperation must have at length driven him mad, for he finally stole me from my father's house by force, slaying all our family and servants before absconding with me to these distant regions. Whether he thought I might submit from either fear or resignation, I know not.

"But I escaped! Slipping free from his clutches, I wandered blindly, knowing myself still hunted, still desired, wondering where I might hope to find sanctuary from his insidious clutches. Then, I heard tell of the fabled Ark of Numynaris, where beauty is shared and venerated in a Frolic unlike anything that has graced the world in all its storied history. And I heard of you, oh gracious host, who in elegance and wisdom stands so far above anyone else. I sought refuge here, a home to call my own after mine had been stolen. How happy I was in this briefest moment aboard! But then I awoke from that bliss to see *him*, his face seeking to drag me back into his horrid embrace. I was so frightened, so succumb to dread, and I did not know what else to do but obey."

With every word Emrasarie offered, Numynaris leaned closer, as if to savor more intimately each detail of the story she wove. Further torment of Uralant was abandoned as Emrasarie allowed her lips to quiver, her voice to falter, and her head to sink low in bashful veneration at precisely the opportune moments, so her audience had eyes for only her; eyes bulging too wide past creaseless lids and sparkling with too vibrant a coruscation of colors. The mask opposite her, so perfect in every other aspect, could no longer hide the yearning for that most essential, yet stubbornly elusive need lurking in the hearts of all entities who breathe, think, and feel. Emrasarie, her own mask fully donned, smiled precisely to stoke the fires of such passion and bring her quarry ever closer still.

"Please," she begged, raising her hands as if to cusp the epicene's face in adoration. "To dwell amidst your splendor is all I wish. There is naught else in this world as your presence, and my heart would shatter to be torn from such beauty. Please, let me lose myself in your touch; in your embrace; in your everything."

Numynaris's face swelled forward, until all the world was eclipsed behind its span. Feeling the soft and stale breath exuded from lips pursed so near to her, Emrasarie craned her head up to reach their glistening contours, while her hand discretely slid to the hidden pocket along her dress.

The moment before they met, Emrasarie grabbed the epicene's collar, holding firm the face atop as best she was able. She then thrust the object she held upwards, the vial of rhogalida venom now uncapped, into the only exposed opening to be found upon her foe.

Numynaris gagged and lurched backwards in shock, trying to grab hold and spit out the swiftly draining ampoule even as it emptied. Thin fingers of rufescent liquid streamed down the epicene's chin, and by the time the glass did drop and shatter upon the floor, it was far too late. No amount of heaving could call back the quantity already imbibed.

A cloud of incomprehension darkened those bulging eyes. Something shimmered there, something cold despite the burning shine they suddenly drew, a mien which Emrasarie surmised its wearer had not known for a long, *long* time: fear.

Before Numynaris could utter even a single word, the venom took hold, and a gurgling wail unlike anything she had ever heard clawed its way up through that gaping mouth. She had seen many times how just a few droplets of the substance could devour through even the toughest, most sinewy of meats given enough time and a sufficient concentration; under the onslaught of an entire vial's worth, she could hardly imagine what ruin the epicene's internal organs were being reduced to now. Instead, she watched with horrified awe the nightmare that was Numynaris flailing about in insane and desperate futility, as no amount of grasping, clutching, and tearing at chest plate or throat could save what had been sealed away so tightly inside from being utterly consumed.

It was with a final pitiful gurgle, wheezed out from a face no longer able to emote the abject agony it endured, that the schema housing what had once been Numynaris went sickeningly limp, and dropped in a hollowed heap to the floor.

Rushing to Uralant's side, Emrasarie thanked all the machinations of ineffable Fate when she saw steady breath, no matter how strained, still flowing out from between his pallid lips. She dropped to her knees then, suddenly aware of how exhausted she truly was, and of how close to the absolute edge of Oblivion, from whose precipice there could be no return from, they had both been brought to. Though the air of that chamber now seethed with thick charnel fumes, the remnants of what had once occupied the fallen orichalcum prison escaping through its smallest and otherwise invisible creases, she cared not, and so lay beside her beloved as sleep began to drape its dark curtain across her eyes.

"Rest now, my love," she whispered, touching Uralant's face, and did not wipe those tears which welled up from within her away. "Rest, and know I will be here with you when you wake."

X

SUNSET spilled through the window above Emrasarie, emblazoning the bed on which Uralant slept with warm and golden hues. She watched intently the calm expression upon his face, vigilant even as fatigue clawed at her own eyes. Stretching slightly, she settled back into the arms of her chair, refusing for the time being to answer the impulse.

Three days had come and gone since their night upon the Ark. Three days since the polished artifice wrapped around the Frolic was ripped apart into tattered ribbons for all Lucrauna to see. Outside the walls of the inn they'd returned to, Emrasarie could hear the same panicked din that had gripped the city uninterrupted for so many hours prior as its autochthons were suddenly forced to grapple with memories now befouled beneath the harsh glare of unwanted and untoward insight.

In truth, she was thankful she no longer had to contend with crowds of so many of the Frolic's past participants thronging back along those banks where its once immaculate veil had been rent asunder. Her own time aboard the Ark, and the subsequent confrontation with the architect behind its façade, still festered as if a freshly cut wound yet to heal, and she did not need further impressions of that same terror added to those already plaguing her from the mouths of strangers.

It was their screams which had stirred her, she shuddered to remember. A chorus of horrified cries echoing down from the garden and into the Ark's lower chamber where she and Uralant lay. Finally were the revelers of that last and final Frolic awake, and without the subtle hand of their usual host to remove in secret all trace of feasting vampyric wires, so had they returned to consciousness from the languor cast upon them with those wicked instruments still pierced into the softness of their flesh.

Stroking gingerly the bandages wrapped around her palms, she thought of the pain each rung of the scaffold tower had inflicted as she'd climbed back up its extent. The lacerations staining red her hands had been enough to make her weep, but it was the thought of leaving Uralant alone down there, the idea that in searching for aide she was somehow abandoning him in so horrid a place, which had nearly compelled her to stop and forgo any further ascent towards the garden above.

For her perseverance, she'd been rewarded upon reaching the portal torn through the cypress's trunk with a scene of half-naked and half-crazed pandemonium. Unheard rang her cries for help amidst the manic flight engaged by the Frolic's prior revelers, the need to escape so revolting a place as the amphitheater had been revealed to be leaving them blind and deaf to all else. Stumbling along in the wake of their procession, Emrasarie soon found herself returned to the deck of the Ark outside, where the terrified crowds had so tightly congregated.

All searching for the gondolas by which they'd initially arrived had ended unsuccessfully, and likewise was the coracle left along the bow by Uralant and Zelaeus nowhere to be seen, no doubt stolen by the first panicked soul to have happened upon its presence. With no means to vacate the structure now floating idly and without purpose along the Amaranthyn, the vast number gathered there along the vessel's rim had begun shouting out as loud as possible in the hopes of hailing someone ashore who might hear them. Safe passage back to the waiting docks ashore was readily given by mercantile and personal craft alike, and it had been only from these new arrivals that Emrasarie finally secured aid in retrieving her beloved from the inner chamber buried so deep beneath the Ark.

Thereafter had the entire city been swept aflame in at last understanding the full horror of the Frolic's purpose.

A knock at the door wrested Emrasarie free from such thoughts. Grateful for the distraction, she smiled upon seeing the matron waiting there at the room's threshold, a small tray of delicacies and cups filled to the brim with tea in hand. She entered, placing the victuals on the seat from which Emrasarie had risen, all the while staring with unmasked awe at Uralant sleeping peacefully on the bed.

"I had to see for myself," she muttered, her voice light with wonder. "Remarkable! His wounds truly have vanished!"

Emrasarie nodded. "I cannot say how much longer he could have held on if she had not found me."

Indeed, though he'd fought every second for the breath that tethered him to this world, the damage done to Uralant's worryingly contorted spine had so often upon their return to Lucrauna seemed too great a burden for him to bear. He had snarled and sobbed through so much pain already, the salves applied by apothecaries proving woefully inadequate in reaching the depths from which his suffering stemmed, offering but temporary illusions of relief, while physicians at their worktables could find no arrangement of assembled splints or bandage rolls able to set right what had so severely been broken. Hope for his recovery had dwindled, Emrasarie having seen him spiral down so many pits of insurmountable agony over and over again, each time finding solace only in the unconscious wasteland always waiting at their ends.

"What did you say her name was?" the matron asked.

"She gave none."

"How odd! Does she not wish others to know it was by her hands such miraculous feats were given form, and thereby receive the renown she would then so rightly earn?"

Emrasarie shrugged. "She seemed unconcerned with praises or rewards. Even when I tried offering what little I had as payment, she still refused."

The matron shook her head, disbelief written plainly across her face. "Perhaps she was one of those ascetics who drift from land to land as if by the wind, holding no place as home and carrying only dreams to their name. She certainly looked the type, no?"

Any definitive answers proved too elusive for their speculations to grasp, though they spoke a while still before the matron left to fulfill her other duties.

Even after everything that had happened, Emrasarie could not truly say how it was she'd come across the old woman they had spoken of, the woman to whom she now owed so much. The desperation after so many repeated failures to heal her beloved had blurred much from that particular span of time. For how long she had floundered through Lucrauna's street seeking aid, she could not say. Into how many doorways she had burst, babbling like a madwoman to so many who couldn't help, and many who would not even if they could, she dared not try and count.

Yet she could never forget the wizened face of the woman who'd suddenly stood opposite her on returning to the exterior of the inn, nor the sensation of unrestrained and boundless hope that had flooded through her when the crone had reached out and gently took her hand.

A frayed and weather-beaten frock had been the extent of her garb, cloaking a figure hunched over and beset by such crippling senescence she could but hobble awkwardly with the support of a cane equally as gnarled as herself. And though in every way she stood so far apart from those flawless droves feasted on through centuries by the Frolic's insatiable appetite, and indeed Emrasarie as well, beauty of a different sort had flared from within her nonetheless, a truth gleaned at by such exquisite rhytids writ across her features, and endless amaurotic eyes beholden not to the transience of the present, but instead those unspoken whispers from the infinite heart. There had been no secrets kept from her then, no fear too inconsequential to remain undivulged, and before Emrasarie had fully grasped what transpired, so had the woman followed her up to the room where Uralant clung precariously to life.

She had leaned over him there, small as a child compared to Uralant even as he lay bedridden, and had brushed back the hair smattered across his sweat-drenched brow. Then, eyes rolling back behind their heavy hoods, the woman's hands had begun to sway through the air, back and forth in pattern, as if directing with the most subtle touches the weaving of invisible and otherwise insubstantial strings.

Emrasarie had nearly exclaimed aloud when an aureole had suddenly wrapped around and encased her beloved, its sublime brightness flaring and receding as if by the insistence of the woman's movement. Unlike the sorcerous feats she had witnessed over the past several days, these came not at the behest of words never meant to slip from the straining mouths of mortal men, but from within the woman herself, as if some hidden font of untapped wonder resided deep within her, and required only the enubilating push of purest empathy in order to be shared.

Soon had Uralant been wreathed in what appeared nothing less than starlight, its luminescence so vibrant she'd had to shield her eyes for fear of being blinded. When at length the coruscation lessened, there remained upon his skin a faint shimmer for several moments still, and which, for reasons Emrasarie could not explain, brought tears to her unbelieving eyes.

Almost immediately was Uralant's anguish lessened. The welts and wounds so elusive to other healing practices were suddenly mended, and he eased into a softer, more restful sleep thereafter. The woman, her breathing heavy from exhaustion, had then turned to Emrasarie and smiled. "He dreams of you," she'd said.

Despite so great an act of thaumaturgy, the woman had left soon after, disappearing back into the bustle of Lucrauna as if she were little more than a phantasm, one who'd been conjured by Emrasarie's refusal to accept the possibility she might lose her beloved. Yet the veracity of that experience was evident there upon the bed, clear for all to see, and she had watched over him all the while, leaving only when the need came to procure food or water for her own well-being.

A sudden cough burst through her mounting fatigue, and brought all attention back to where Uralant lay.

"Where...are we? What...what happened?" he asked, voice fragile as fabric pulled apart to its very last strand.

Nearly flinging herself to the bedside, Emrasarie threw her arms around her beloved's shoulders, relief spilling out as tears upon her face. "Hush now, my love; you are safe. Trouble yourself not with such concerns. We are returned to Lucrauna, and free at last from the enemies who sought our destruction."

Confusion still burning within his eyes, Emrasarie tried as best she could to recount all that had transpired, from the manner in which Numynaris had at last been defeated to his own miraculous recovery here in this room. When she had concluded, Uralant sat quiet for a moment, before he leaned back into the pillow and let his eyes wander to some distant, nebulous area overhead. "Stupid," he sighed, still weak, but already regained much of his former tenor.

Taken aback, Emrasarie made to touch her beloved's brow, fearing some fever might have found its way inside and made him delirious. Instead, he took her hand in his and met her eyes with a tired smile. "I should have guessed," he continued. "I should have known a practitioner of sorcery would not be so lax in safe-guarding something they believed to be precious. Now, we have naught but bruises and an aching head to show for all our efforts."

It took Emrasarie a moment to realize she was laughing. She shook her head, and smoothed the mane of dark hair trailing wildly down Uralant's face, smiling all the while in return.

"We need but be patient to see fortune swing back in our favor, no? Tell me, my love; upon whose burdensome and over-ripened purse should we strike next?"

About the Author

Chase A. Folmar is a writer of speculative fiction, especially in the vein of weird fantasy and horror. A graduate of the University of North Carolina at Asheville, he currently lives in Virginia with his wife and their horde of rescued pets. You can find all of his writings and other projects on his website, www.chaseafolmar.com.